There Was A Time

BY

Kenneth Neff Hammontree

There Was A Time

There Was A Time

Published by Living History Productions
302 Center Street, Ashland, Ohio, 44805

Printed by BookMasters, Inc. 2541 Ashland Road,
Mansfield, Ohio 44905

Cover Design by Dianne Spreng
Ashland, Ohio

Library of Congress Control Number: 2004111603
ISBN 0-9761327-0-2
(Formerly ISBN 0-8062-5372-X)

Dedication

There was a Time is dedicated to those fortunate few who have experienced what real love is all about. After all, is it not better to have loved and lost, than never to have loved at all?

Author's Note

The story you are about to read is based on the romance of 20-year-old Mary Virginia "Jennie" Wade, the only civilian killed during the three-day Battle of Gettysburg, and her sweetheart, Corporal Jack Skelly, who died from wounds received at the battle of Carter's Woods, Virginia, outside of Winchester. No one can know for certain what Jack Skelly or Jennie Wade was thinking, or what he or she actually said in the past, unless it had been written down or dictated to another. With that in mind the author has taken the liberty of creating dialogue between the characters in this historical Civil War romance novel. The author has also taken the liberty of adding fictional characters along with the historical ones. With the exception of the historical characters, places, and dates some of the characters in the novel are fictitious and any resemblance to living persons, present or past, is coincidental.

July 10, 2004
Kenneth Neff Hammontree

1
The Longing
April 14, 1863

As the bright sun rose over the gentle, rolling countryside surrounding the small borough of Gettysburg, it brought with it the birth of a new day. The gathering light permeated the expanses of winter wheat, its warmth transforming the wooded hillsides of poplar, elm, and hickory into cathedrals of illuminating golden rays. Slowly, as the gray shadows gave way and the morning mist began rising between the dark green ridges and shallow valleys, the promise of a warm day flooded the countryside

Jennie had been awake long before the sun's rays pierced the small-framed window of her bedroom and cast their hazy light onto the oak floor, worn with age. Lying there in the walnut spindle bed that once belonged to her grandmother; she could hear the distant, familiar sounds of the early morning as they began filling her room with their presence.

Spring had arrived earlier this year than in previous years, and with it came the warmest April anyone in Gettysburg could remember.

The anticipation of a bountiful fall harvest was in everyone's conversation, especially the farmers of surrounding Adams County, Pennsylvania.

Even without the excellent weather of early spring the farmers and merchants of Adams County would have been busy. However, with this April warm spell the farmers and merchants were up earlier than normal, performing the morning chores and getting a good start on the day.

Jennie's daily struggle this spring had been dealing with the annoying clatter from these ever-increasing morning activities just outside her bedroom window. As far as she was concerned, the noise meant only one thing to her: loss of a good night's sleep, which resulted in those cursed dark lines under her eyes, leading her to believe that she would become less attractive to men in general, and to her childhood friend Corporal Jack Skelly in particular.

Stretching her arms in an effort to remove the stiffness of the night's sleep from her body, she inhaled a deep breath of fresh morning air. I'm so happy we don't live on a farm, she thought; as she expelled the air from her lungs with a long drawn-out sigh. I just can't see myself getting up at this ungodly hour every morning for the rest of my life, and if I were a farmer's wife, that is exactly what I would be a-doing. Why, even God Almighty Himself is still sleeping at this hour, she thought, as her small oval mouth formed a faint smile. However, the smile left her face as quickly as it appeared when she again heard the ringing of the anvil at the nearby blacksmith's shop.

"Heaven only knows being a tailor's daughter is bad enough with the workload and such these days," she whispered to herself as she drew the sheet over her head and closed her eyes.

"Why, I just don't know what I would do if I would become the wife of Jack Skelly after this here terrible war gets itself over, and Jack takes up dirt farming as a living," she exclaimed with an assertiveness in her voice.

"Yes, I would just divorce that man," she chirped, weighing each word cautiously. "That's exactly what I would do to that rascal Jack Skelly, if he would take up farming," she said in a resolute voice as she pushed the sheet down to her legs and then folded her arms across her chest. She paused for a few moments looking out the window and listened to a passing wagon on Breckenridge Street below. "Then, again, I may never marry that man, even if he pursues me," she whispered cautiously knowing the real answer was buried deep in her heart.

She could hear the chimes of the kitchen mantel clock downstairs striking five o'clock. It was useless to remain in bed trying to get back to sleep. She knew the needed sleep would refuse to come to her. Her mind and heart were much too full; filled with thoughts of Jack and his homecoming. She tossed aside the tangled bed sheet over her legs and turned over on her stomach, burying her head deep in the pillow as her nightgown spread across the bed. Her thoughts, enmeshed in the week ahead, were caught in a swirling, racing whirlwind with no relief in sight. Emotions and thoughts were spinning in useless circles as Jennie tried to focus on the day's work ahead.

Jack will be home tonight and then I shall see what happens. Yes, I will find out what his true intentions really are toward me. A smile appeared on her face as she thought more intently on Jack's homecoming, and this thought stimulated the anticipation that had been building up for weeks. Ever since she had received Jack's last letter in early March informing her of his leave beginning the week of April 14, she could hardly wait for his return.

I could feel much better about a whole lot of other things in my life if I knew how he was going to respond to me, she thought. Will he be warm and friendly toward me, or cold and distant? He certainly knows how to be both around me, she thought. Who knows, I just may refuse his attentions in calling on me this week; after all when he left for this stupid war in November he just left me hanging out there on a limb. In fact, the six letters I got from him throughout the winter have not given me any clue at all as to where I will fit into his life.

She slowly got up, sat on the edge of the bed, removed the six letters from underneath the corn mattress and placed them on the walnut nightstand. For a few moments she just looked at the letters. "How will he respond to me?" she said, gently picking up the fragile pile of brown worn letters. "Will he propose? Hmm! I just don't know." Intently Jennie began looking over each individual letter that had been sent from Camp Buehler, and then opened the last one Jack sent. "Dear Miss Wade…" She paused and shook her head. "He would always begin his letters this way," she whispered to herself. "Why wasn't he more clear in his writings as to his intentions?" she said in a disquieted, questioning voice. The six letters, which she read every day until they became so worn they could no longer be opened without tearing the center of the page, had not given her any insight into their relationship other than they were very close friends, and his admiration for her was great. However, this reluctance to propose or commit to Jennie in any form before he left for Camp Buehler exasperated her to no end, and because of his reluctance she would vacillate back and forth on her thoughts of what action to take with him.

"Gettysburg is a large borough, and there are plenty of places where I can go to avoid Jack if I so desire," she said in an anguished voice. However, deep within her heart she knew her love and devotion for Jack would always draw her to him. Jennie's heart began beating faster with thoughts of Jack's arrival this evening at the train station. She paused for a few moments, and tried to search for the correct response to this excitement. Startled at this unsettling revelation, Jennie rolled back onto the bed trying to regain her composure.

She loved him.

She always had.

She always would.

"I wish I knew if Jack loves me as much as I love him," she questioned with a sigh.

Ever since their school days together she had felt an attraction toward him, and believed Jack had the same feelings. One time in the schoolyard when they were in the sixth grade,

Jack took her aside and told her he believed that they would be together, forever.

Forever, she thought. How foolish she had been to believe Jack could be in love with her, and that it would be forever. Why, there is nothing that is forever.

She sometimes felt that real love was something that would happen to someone else, but never her. And because of this belief, her feeling of losing Jack had grown insensibly over the past winter, as each letter would be examined thoroughly for anything that would communicate a sign of affection. Or anything in his words that hinted they would be together, forever.

"Mary Virginia, come on now it's way past time for you to be getting up," her mother Mary Wade called from downstairs. "You know that Captain Black will be a coming to get his uniform this evening. Now make haste, girl," she reiterated, only this time in a stronger voice.

Now, who really cares about Captain Black's dumb uniform, Jennie thought mischievously to herself as she slid out of bed. "For heaven's sake, Mother, you would think by your voice that Captain Black was old Abe Lincoln himself coming to get his uniform," Jennie shouted down to her mother.

Mrs. Wade paid little attention to what her daughter said and continued stacking the firewood in the kitchen wood box for the morning meal. Mrs. Wade had always acted as if Jenny was downright lazy; however: anyone that knew Jennie understood that this was just not true. Hard work had been profoundly instilled in her from birth, through a long line of industrious German parentage.

At only five feet two inches tall, Jennie was considered average height for the women of her times. She was petite, and solid, and except for her large bosom, looked rather small in stature to her friends and family. However, it was her strong character and determination that made up for anything that she lacked in size. Her long thick hair was the color of lucid coal. Jennie preferred to part it in the middle, with a long braid surrounding her perfectly oval face. Her lively dark blue eyes, fringed with long black lashes, expressed a definite inner strength. Her mother always told her that she had inherited her father's eyes, as well as his stubborn will. But, it had been that tenacious will that enabled Jennie to maintain their home all these years, along with her mother's assistance. Jennie entered into young adulthood accepting her place in keeping the family together, and accomplished this without the moral and financial support of her father.

With the coming of the Civil War, Jennie and her mother had more than they could handle with the additional workload of repairing army uniforms for the local soldiers and merchants. The tailoring work doubled after Lincoln's call to arms, and both Mary Wade and Jennie found themselves working 10-hour days just to keep up with the volume of uniforms.

In spite of this tremendous work burden, Jennie found time for her quiet walks around town window-shopping. The walks were good for her, allowing the time necessary for reflection, and, if nothing else, time away from her work and her brothers. In the winter of 1862, the 10th New York Cavalry Regiment, called the "Porter Guards," was stationed in Gettysburg for a three-month period. The soldiers spent all that winter in military drilling. It appeared to Jennie that it was from the day the "Porter Guards" came to town until now that their workload had increased.

After finishing with her sponge bath and slipping on her light brown day dress with the dark ruffles gathered at the bottom, Jennie walked over to the large oval standing mirror and stared intently at the reflection as she gathered her long black hair over her head. "I wonder if Jack will like my hair up in a French knot," she said in a murmured voice. She had remembered what Mary Comfort shared in church a few weeks ago: the latest fashion from Europe was the French knot.

Jennie stood there staring into the mirror as if mesmerized by her own reflection, and played with her hair. Her long, loosened, black hair flowed over her shoulders and partly covered her large full breasts. Closing her eyes Jennie tried to imagine what it would be like tonight when she saw Jack for the first time in six months. The thought of him filled her with a warm sensation that pulsated through her entire body. It was a sensation like no other she had ever experienced.

From downstairs Jennie could hear her brothers, Samuel and Harry, laughing and carrying on in the kitchen. From the sound of the conversation, Jennie knew she had better finish dressing and get down to the kitchen as soon as possible, for a fight was surely coming.

As Jennie entered the kitchen, Samuel and Harry were making fun of their older brother John's small stature. In teasing John, who was only five feet three inches tall, the brothers would always bring up the fact that the Union Army did not make a uniform small enough for John to wear. Therefore, the brothers concluded,

John would be the only son in the entire Wade family who would not be able to fight the Rebs. Of course John would always become infuriated at being teased about his stature. Sometimes the bantering between the brothers would go on for hours until a fight would ensue.

John James, who was 17, had been trying to get his mother's permission to enlist in the Pennsylvania Volunteers as a bugler boy. Both Jennie and her mother had been discouraging him from enlisting for months. However, Jennie was almost certain that in a few months John would be riding out of Gettysburg heading into this terrible war and a possible young death.

John's desire to enlist in the army was stimulated and encouraged by all of the talk lately of a Confederate invasion into Pennsylvania. The local talk around town was that the Rebs could be as close as York, Harrisburg, or New Oxford, which would bring the war to the very doorsteps of Gettysburg. John envied his stepbrother James, the only child from their father's first marriage, so much that it had become an overpowering compulsion for him to join the army as soon as possible.

James had enlisted in 1861. He was with the Third Pennsylvania heavy artillery with a rank of corporal. At the present time, James was stationed at Fortress Monroe and had been sending home letters, which filled John's mind with visions of grandeur, glory, and romance of war.

At least Jennie did not have to worry about Samuel and young Harry going off to war. By the time they would be old enough to enlist, this godless, bloody war of rebellion would be over. She believed both Samuel and Harry had the potential and the ability to do well in school and at home if only given a chance. Because of this belief, Jennie had always hoped that the boys would be given a better chance in life very different from the one she and Georgia experienced growing up.

The brothers were typical young boys and once in awhile would find themselves in some type of trouble, either at school or home. A few weeks ago John placed a rather large black rat snake in the teacher's desk with the help of Samuel. Needless to say, the little joke gave both brothers an early leave from school and some time off, which delighted both boys. Early in the spring 12-year-old Samuel found a job as a delivery boy for Mr. Pierce's butcher shop. The shop was just at the end of Breckenridge Street on the southeast corner of the intersection of Baltimore Street. Samuel stayed with the Pierces on the days and weekends he was needed for delivering and packaging meat. This helped in getting Samuel away from his brothers and out of trouble. Samuel was paid with meat, adding to the family support. However, the days that Samuel was home from the Pierces, the trouble between the brothers would occasionally rear up its ugly head.

There were many times over the past few years that Jennie had wished her younger sister, Martha Margaret, would have lived to help her raise Samuel and Harry. Martha died in 1849, leaving Jennie and Georgia with the responsibility of caring for and supporting the family. Then last April 15, 1862, Georgia married John McClellan, which created an added workload for Jennie at home. Yet, in spite of the many difficulties, the family had survived financially and together as a whole family. Fortunately, none of her brothers so far had been lost to the war, and Jennie daily prayed none would.

Watching her brothers at the kitchen table, Jennie thought that God had truly shone his grace upon their family. Jennie remembered one of Jack's first letters this past winter, when an incident occurred in Virginia. His company had captured some Rebs and was shocked to learn that the "enemy" they had been fighting over the last several weeks was made up of 10 and 12-year-olds. As Jennie sat there at the kitchen table she became more determined to keep her younger brothers from such a terrible fate. How sad their mothers must feel, not knowing where their sons are, she thought as she shook her head.

Her mother entered the kitchen and walked over to the cook stove that was radiating with heat and poured the hot mix into the pan on the stove. The kitchen was exceptionally hot and humid, and Jennie opened both windows to let in the cool morning breeze, making the kitchen more tolerable to work in. She checked the woodbin, making sure there was enough wood for the day's cooking, and saw that it would need more fuel. She then sat down at the table across from her brothers while the hot cakes were cooking.

Without looking up at Jennie, Mary Wade questioned her daughter. "So, will you be a-seeing that Skelly boy tonight?"

"Yes mother, I will be meeting him at the train station." Jennie replied.

"Jennie, you know I don't approve of that Skelly boy or his white trash family. I know I can't stop you from seeing him, but I am telling you right now that that boy is not allowed in this house, and...." She paused as if she had something else to add.

"And remember that boy is not allowed on the house porch either! Do you understand Jennie?" She thundered across the room. The kitchen became quiet as the boys looked at Jennie for her answer.

However, Jennie did not answer, pretending not to hear her mother's cutting words. The comments were not new to her or her brothers. Jennie had heard the disparaging remarks about her relationship with Jack many times over in the past six months. The remarks began as soon as her mother found out she was corresponding with him.

The room remained silent for what seemed like hours as the clock ticked away the moments.

"You know, they said at school last Friday that old man Lee and his Reb army is on the move down in Virginia and heading toward Pennsylvania," Samuel chirped across, the table breaking cold silence. "It's bad times for our state. Old Man Lee is going to cross into our state and there is nothing that we can do about it." He paused to see if anyone in the room was listening to his doomsday message.

"Everyone at school is excited that they might have a chance to get their licks in."

Observing that he now had captured everyone's attention, he continued. "My teacher, who knows a lot about this-here war because of his son in the army, says that Lee has a hundred thousand men coming our way. My teacher also said...."

"Now, just you hold on to your britches, Samuel," Jennie said after reaching a point when she could no longer remain silent. "I believe your teacher is spinning a tall yarn when it comes to the number of Rebs in Lee's army." Jennie wiped the perspiration from her forehead and continued. "The last letter that I read from Jack Skelly said there was only about 75,000 in the Reb army and they...."

"Well, I don't care what you have heard from that Jack Skelly man of yours," Samuel said, interrupting. "There are thousands of Rebs, and they are coming our way. And, I am a-thinking our boys in blue will whip them real good, like...." Samuel paused as if searching for the words to corroborate his remarks, and then continued, "Whip then real good-like, with my help of course," he chuckled.

Jennie decided not to continue the conversation. She knew all too well that these Rebs so far in this war had outfought, outwitted, and in general "beat the pants off" the boys in blue. She shook her head thinking about how many commanding generals the North had had; more generals than the fleas on a dog's back in mid-July. Ever since the battle of Bull Run, when the North had great visions of destroying the Confederacy in one swift blow, it had been difficult to win just one battle. But how do you tell young boys about that? She thought as she looked at her brothers sitting across from her at the table. They would never believe a woman anyway, especially their sister.

"That's enough war talk," Mary Wade announced in a stern and impatient voice. "Now you boys go get your buckwheat cakes tended to and then go fetch more wood in for the box." She turned and looked directly at Jennie. "Yes, there had been enough war talk this morning for a lifetime." Her mother's look was cold and distant.

The tension between Jennie and her mother had increased daily since last November. Mary Wade had always felt that the Skelly family was "white trash" and tried to persuade Jennie not to have anything to do with the family or Jack. These emotions originated with the problems encountered by Mary's husband James Wade a few years back.

Jennie wanted to look the other way, but refused to allow her mother to interfere with her personal life. This was a promise she had made to herself over a year ago, and so far she had kept it by not allowing her mother to control her life, like the matriarch had for the other children in the family.

Jennie finished her breakfast of hotcakes and applesauce and quietly sat there, drinking her coffee and listening to her brothers bantering back and forth as they carried in the stove wood. There was so much to do today that Jennie did not know where to begin. Her mother came back into the kitchen and helped Jennie with the morning dishes and reminded her to pick up little Isaac Brinkerhoff before she began her day. Jennie quickly washed the kitchen table and mopped the hard wood floors before leaving for the Brinkerhoff residence.

Isaac Brinkerhoff was a young crippled boy whom the Wades had accepted as a boarder while his mother worked during the day. Isaac was not physically deformed, but simply had difficulty in walking without help and could not take care of himself. Caring for little Isaac assisted in contributing to the overall financial health of the Wade family. On returning home with Isaac, Jennie began her seamstress work with the completion of Captain Black's uniform and the other uniforms that her mother had stacked on the oak table in the front parlor.

By mid-afternoon Jennie had completed not only Captain Black's uniform, but also five others. Her attention now turned to the work on her special dress, which she kept on the mannequin in the corner of the parlor. Jennie had begun working on the dress six months ago when Jack left, and wanted to have it completed by the time he came home.

Georgia had acquired two high-quality crinolines, and had given one of them to Jennie. They were made out of whalebone instead of wire, which was less expensive. The crinoline was exactly what Jennie had always wanted but never dared hope for, and was curious as to how Georgia obtained them, but never asked.

It was Georgia who also gave her the ribbons of blue lace for her dress, which was purchased in Hanover. When Jennie asked how she could repay her, Georgia simply replied, "Maybe someday I can wear your dress to a dance with my John." Both of them laughed, knowing that the good Lord created Jennie a little more endowed than Georgia.

Georgia had always shared with her sister, and Jennie would never forget her unselfish kindness in the past. Even though there had been times over the years that Georgia had been jealous of Jennie, it was just part of the growing up competition of sisters.

Looking out her small bedroom window, Jennie could see the lengthening shadows of evening begin to descend across Breckenridge

Street. Standing there by her bedroom window, a profound melancholy feeling that had been gathering all day overwhelmed her with a charged emotion. This feeling had begun with the reading of Jack's letters and continued to encompass her throughout the day.

Slowly, Jennie began to freshen up before leaving for the train station. She wanted to allow herself enough time to walk down to her sister's house just south of town on Baltimore Pike.

"I'm hoping Georgia feels well enough to walk with me to the train station," she whispered to herself as she combed out her long black hair, and then brought it up on her head, forming an oval frame. Georgia had been in a family way for five months now, but still walked everywhere around town.

Jennie just felt uncomfortable walking uptown to the train station without an escort. But if the truth were really known, Jennie was very apprehensive about seeing Jack. It was as if she were beginning a perilous journey into the unknown and needed reassurance. She was anxious; anxious to know the real truth of Jack's innermost feelings toward her.

Jennie walked back to the bedroom window, stood there and looked across to the street below. As evening settled in, the streets were quieted down.

She wanted to believe he cared.

She wanted to hope for the best.

She just had to know if Jack loved her.

A tear appeared in the corner of her eye, and she wiped it away as soon as she felt its wetness on her cheek. She had no idea where it came from. In the distance, the haunting sound of a whippoorwill rose above the clatter of a single passing buggy from Breckenridge Street below. Again, the melancholy emotion overwhelmed her accompanied by a deep sense of loneliness and longing.

She wanted the emotions to leave, but they would not. She wanted peace about her relationship with Jack, but it eluded her.

"In the place of crying," Jennie said to herself in a soft murmured voice, "oftentimes, there are hurts, sorrows, and longings that lie too deep, even for human tears."

2
The Train Station
April 14, 1863

Although the birth of her child was only four months away, Georgia was still working late into the evening. Holding her kitchen door open with a bare foot, she brought in the final load of seasoned wood for the evening meal and morning breakfast from the woodshed behind the brick house. She carried the wood over to the cast iron stove in the east corner of the kitchen under the stairs. Georgia's husband John had carefully cut the wood for his wife, and made sure it was thoroughly dried to give off the best heat for cooking.

Along with her other daily chores, bringing in the cooking wood was something she would tolerate until John came home from the war. After their marriage a year ago, John had been with her for only a little over a month before he left for the army. Since then she had only seen him on a few brief furloughs. In John's absence, Georgia had found herself not only the breadwinner, but responsible for all of the daily chores. There were days, however, like this one, when she was so discouraged about missing John that Georgia was sorry she did not wait until the war was over before marrying him.

To be in a family way and not have her husband around to share in the joys and wonders of his growing child within her was very difficult. She knew that she only had herself to blame. Georgia had been fully aware of what she was getting into when they were married, and knew her husband would be leaving in a few weeks. And no one but the Almighty knew if he would ever return to her. Love was strong in their hearts and Georgia wanted to get married before he left. Now she had second thoughts. However, at the time she saw the marriage as a way of being on her own and getting out of an unhappy situation at home.

Both Georgia and John were born in Gettysburg and grew up together, attending the same school. John Louis spent most of his childhood days playing in the McClellan Hotel, which had been in the McClellan family going back to 1808.

As the years passed, they became childhood sweethearts. Georgia could remember that even in childhood all John ever talked about was that someday he wanted to become a soldier.

On April 20, 1861, John's childhood dream became a reality when he answered President Lincoln's first call for volunteers. John was enrolled at the Pennsylvania College, but never thought twice about leaving college to join up. At the end of the first 90 days, he enlisted for a longer period of time with the first 165th Pennsylvania Infantry Regiment, Company E. Three months before they were married, on April 15, 1862, John mustered in for another nine months. However, he did manage to obtain a one-week furlough between his services for their wedding.

That same week they decided to rent a small but very cozy one-and-a-half-story double red brick dwelling. It had been built around 1820, according to the locals, and was constructed in a Dutch Colonial style, with an overjet on each side. It was built for two families, one on the north side and one on the south side. There was also a beautiful white lattice fence at the street level, on top of a fieldstone retaining wall, with fieldstone steps up to the house. A white picket fence on the east and west sides of the house divided the yard, which was filled with fruit trees. The house was everything that Georgia had ever dreamed about as a little girl.

The only thing that bothered her was the fact that the house was located just southeast from the Snider Wagon Tavern and Hotel at the base of East Cemetery Hill on the East Side of Baltimore Pike. The Tavern Hotel dominated the area where Baltimore Pike and Emmitsburg Road came together. She had been concerned about the possibility of noise from the Tavern in the evening. As time went by, the noise was a concern that never became a reality.

The house was a place where Georgia and John could call their own. It would be a home where Georgia could get away from the problems at Breckenridge Street between Jennie and their mother. Georgia always tried to remain neutral in the confrontations about the Skellys between her mother and sister, but there were some times when it was unavoidable. Now that she was married, her life centered on her husband John, the war and her coming baby.

In retrospect, her first year of marriage had passed rather quickly, with Georgia spending the majority of the time separated from her husband. At first she believed that she could make the adjustment to the long periods of separation from her husband, and maybe under conditions other than the war she might have. However, with the continuation of the war, each day was lived with the real possibility of notification of his death. John's potential loss was a reality Georgia could never become accustomed to nor accept.

After placing the load of wood in the box, Georgia sat down at the cherry kitchen table John's family had given to them as a wedding gift. This was the first time since early morning that she had had an opportunity to relax. Her kitchen was scented with her favorite fragrances of fresh cloves, cinnamon and hot steaming coffee. The soft glow from the table lamp gave off radiant warmth that permeated the entire room with a sense of security. It was this warm security that Georgia needed at this time in her life.

Leaning back in the kitchen chair, she closed her eyes; holding both hands on her protruding abdomen, she felt her unborn child move. Georgia knew that his birth would not be long in coming. "Such a miracle," she whispered to herself. "If only John could be here at this very moment to feel his son." Georgia had always felt that the good Lord had given them assurance from the moment she became aware that she was in a family way that it would be a boy.

Pouring herself another fresh cup of hot coffee, Georgia leaned back in the chair and warmed her hands, listening to the mesmerizing ticking of the mantel clock. She closed her eyes and began to drift into a light sleep thinking about where her John would be sleeping tonight.

Just as she began to drift off, a quick, repeated knock came from the door. Startled, Georgia jumped up, almost spilling her coffee. "Now, what on earth would Jennie be wanting at this time of day?" she muttered in a questioning voice as she made her way to the door.

Georgia knew by the pattern of knocks that Jennie was responsible. Opening the door, she said in an irritable, but inquisitive voice, "Jennie, what in heaven's name could you be a-wanting at this hour?" Georgia wanted to be angry. She had been irritable long before Jennie came to her door. If there was one thing that she did not need this evening it was talking to anyone. All Georgia wanted was to be left alone, and had it been any other person other than family she would not have answered the door.

Immediately, Jennie could tell by Georgia's voice that she was upset by her sister's unannounced presence. "You know, Jennie, that a young woman does not walk the streets at this hour unescorted." She paused, realizing that by the look on Jennie's face her words were falling on deaf ears. Georgia shook her head and motioned for her sister to enter.

Georgia, at first, thought that Jennie had obtained information about John. Her heart sank when Jennie began talking about some irrelevant topic, which had nothing to do with her husband. "Well, Jennie, what brings you down here at this hour of the evening?" Georgia said impatiently as they both sat down at the table.

"I know that it is not the weather because it has been just fine and I know now that it is not about John. So what is it?"

Jennie paused for a moment to wipe her flushed forehead and face. The suspense was building with every passing moment, as Georgia tried to conceal her excitement.

"Well, George..." Jennie had always called her sister by this name when she was excited or had something important to share with her.

"I need your help this evening. Would you walk with me to the train station? I would like for you to be with me when Jack comes in tonight."

Jennie paused for a moment and looked at the clock. "Now you don't have to, but I..."

"All right Jennie, now just slow down. You mean you want me to be with you when you meet Jack at the train station? Does Mother know about this?" Jennie gave a long sigh and said in a cracked voice, "yes."

"Well, what did she say about you fetching yourself up to the station to see Jack?" Georgia questioned in a tense voice.

Jennie explained, "Mother said in no uncertain terms and such that Jack was not allowed on our property. And even if she said that I could not go, you know Georgia that I would."

"Why didn't you tell me this past Sunday after church? Something as important as Jack coming in on leave and you couldn't even share this with your only sister?"

Jennie could tell by her words and tone that Georgia was hurt.

"Please don't be angry, George. I would have told you, if Mother had not been with us. You know she follows me around like a lost puppy dog," Jennie related in a sarcastic voice. "I wanted to tell you all about this exciting news more than anything because you have been the one person who understands my feelings about Jack. I am sorry George."

"Nothing to be sorry about. You know that I understand. We both know that Mother can be very unreasonable at times, about anything and everything." Georgia paused and looked at the clock. "Well we better get started if you plan to be there when his train comes in." Jennie clasped her sister's hand and held it tight for a few moments. "Thanks, George." Jennie said in a voice filled with gratitude.

The night air was crisp and the sky clear as the two began their walk up Baltimore Pike to the Town Square, as the first stars began to twinkle through the increasing darkness.

Georgia could sense the excitement in her sister and yet at the same time, a foreboding presence that surrounded her. Georgia knew of the six letters Jennie had received; however Jennie never revealed their contents to anyone, fearing that it might get back to her mother. And out of respect to Jennie, Georgia never asked.

As they arrived at the train station, the gaslights had just been turned on and were flickering in the gentle breeze, bathing the old building in eerie glow. The air inside the station was permeated with the smells of aged leather and stale cigar smoke.

The room was crowded with people milling about, waiting impatiently for the arrival of the train loaded with troops coming home on leave. A clerk informed them the train was running about 20 minutes behind the scheduled arrival. The young women walked over to a long slender oak bench, worn smooth with years of use, and sat down. From the bench they would be able to see the train coming down the track toward the station.

Jennie, as well as Georgia, never liked coming to the station since the war began over two years ago. The building was a constant reminder to them and to the rest of the town of the ever-growing casualties of the war. What bothered Jennie the most were the coffins that were removed from the boxcars and stacked on the walkway along the building, filled with fallen soldiers waiting for delivery to their final resting place.

As they waited, the station began to fill up with more people, and the air in the small building became warm and very humid. For Georgia, the wait was becoming unbearable as she sat there fanning herself. She needed to get out into the evening air away from the confined station and wanted Jennie to go with her. Jennie, almost crazed with anticipation, refused to move from her vantage point on the bench, fearing that if they went out of the building Jack's train would arrive.

Georgia thought that it would be impossible to miss a noisy large black train pulling into the station. Looking at Jennie Georgia noticed that her cheeks were becoming flushed. "Would you like to use my fan?" Georgia said as she began to wave it gently in front of Jennie's face. "I reckon it would not look good for you to be fainting and on the floor when Jack steps off the train," Georgia laughed.

Before Jennie could reply, they heard in the distance the haunting sound of a train whistle. Immediately, Jennie stood up, and strained her neck, looking in the direction of the sound of the whistle. Her heart began to race wildly in rapid beats. Georgia stood at the same time but could not see anything because of the people gathered in front of them. When she turned to look at Jennie her sister was standing on the bench. Georgia smiled and remembered that exciting day the previous year when John's train came in, and how she felt waiting there at the same station.

Slowly, they began to work their way through the crowd to the large gate at the end of the boardwalk. The train whistle blew again, and the people who had been waiting for hours surged forward, waving their greetings. The moment Jennie had been waiting for all these months finally had arrived. Standing there waiting out the last few minutes her palms began to sweat and her heart pounded inside her chest.

Jennie clasped her arm around Georgia's. "You know George, I feel like running back to my house. I want to see him, then again I don't!" Emotions Jennie had never experienced before now began to overwhelm her.

"Will he look the same, George? Will I know him? Will he be polite to me or take me in his arms and kiss me?" Georgia squeezed Jennie's hand more tightly as they were caught up in the mass of people and pushed forward. Billows of gray steam engulfed the train as it came to a slow stop. A conductor covered in a light, white dust, stepped down in front of the gate. He politely asked the assemblage of people crowded around the gate to please step back. As the people receded, the doors of the cars slid open and soldiers began appearing in the doorways.

Jennie immediately scanned the five cars as the soldiers jumped down to the boardwalk, looking for Jack's face. Over the last six months she had methodically memorized his aristocratic face, with its deep-blue eyes, thick, black unruly hair and his broad smile. She could never forget what Jack looked like, not in a thousand years.

The train cars were just about empty when Jennie thought she saw Jack jumped down from the car and onto the boardwalk with two other soldiers. "Georgia do you see him? Do you see him?" Jennie erupted in a loud voice as she pointed to the group of three soldiers walking toward them.

As the three were walking, Jack was looking around for his brother, Dan Skelly. He had sent his family a letter three weeks ago telling them of the day and time he would arrive in Gettysburg, and wanted Dan to pick him up. His two friends bid him good-bye and strolled away with their families, leaving Jack standing alone but surrounded by people catching up on home news.

"Are you sure that is Jack?" Georgia said, looking intently at the soldier standing now only 20 yards from them. "I do believe that he has up and got him a mustache Jennie."

"Yes I sure believe you are right" Jennie said, working her way toward the isolated soldier standing there listening to the conversations taking place around him. And then there was his broad smile.

As she walked toward him, she remembered the day in school when the class was playing in the back of the schoolyard and she had climbed into a large oak tree to free a kitten that had become stranded on a long limb. Her dress became snagged on a small protruding branch in her endeavor to reach the kitten. She tried to pull it free and lost her balance. Fortunately for Jennie, Jack was watching nearby and saw what was about to happen. Running over to the tree, he caught her just before she landed on the ground. Jennie could still feel the warmth and security of his strong arms around her and the embarrassment of the boy holding her.

"His face and smile, even with that mustache, are still as attractive as the day I first met him at school," Jennie whispered to herself.

"Are you sure Jack does not know you are here? He seems to be looking around intently for someone," Georgia questioned. "Maybe he is looking for someone special in his life?"

"That would be me!" Jennie affirmed in a strong voice, surprised at her own vehemence.

She noticed his uniform was dusty and muddy. He had lost some weight, maybe 10 pounds, and his thick black hair was, like always, in disarray. Overall, Jack looked like he was in good spirits and in good health.

Jennie began to walk slowly toward the small group of soldiers that had gathered around Jack as he stood there waiting. As he talked to his friends, he casually scanned the crowd as if looking for a friendly face.

At first Jennie thought Jack might be looking for her, but she realized he had no idea she was going to meet him this evening. This was exactly what Jennie wanted to do. Surprise him!

Georgia turned and walked back to the bench. She had been standing for most of the day and by now her legs were beginning to feel like two large logs. Besides, she did not want to interfere. Once again, Georgia remembered how she felt when John came home, and she began to cry silently. They were tears of joy for Jennie and tears of sadness for missing her John.

Jennie continued moving slowly toward Jack until she was about 10 feet away from him. His back was toward her as he talked with a fellow soldier. He then suddenly turned, laughing, looking directly in Jennie's direction. Her body froze in place as if paralyzed. For a brief moment his eyes searched across the station overlooking Jennie. Then, his gaze fell upon her, standing there before him like a stone stature. At first Jack thought she was someone else, and was just about to move on, when he realized this woman standing before him was Jennie Wade.

His broad smile disappeared at once and his jaw dropped open as he took a step backwards in disbelief.

"Jennie, Jennie Wade. What on earth are you doing here?" Jack bellowed out. "You are the last person on this earth I thought would be here tonight," he said working his way toward her. "I was expecting to see Dan, not you. Are you taking his place?" He paused for a moment, looking intently into her eyes. "What a pleasant surprise this is."

Jack quickly looked her over, basking in her warm presence. Let me see, how long as it been, he thought to himself.

The same bewitching gaze locking them together by some invisible, magnetic force in the universe had also mesmerized Jennie. Her inner soul had been touched and all of her doubts had vanished like the morning fog over the horizon. She wanted to cry, but dare not in front of Jack.

"Yes, this is quite the surprise," Jack chuckled, breaking the uncomfortable silence. He brought his body close to hers, and she could smell the dust and stale dirt on his uniform. She wanted to move close to Jack, but could not. She closed her eyes as he pulled her tight up against his body and slipped his arms around her waist. She held her breath.

"How I have missed you, Jennie."

"I have missed you, too, Jack Skelly. Yes, I have really missed you too."

Jack pulled her closer to his body sensing their souls were once again reunited as one.

"Now, don't you dare..." Before Jennie could stop him, his warm lips pressed hard against hers. Jennie felt her body surrendering to him and instinctively pulled back.

"Jack Skelly, what in tarnation has gotten hold of you?"

Jack said nothing and pulled her back into his strong arms.

Jennie did not know what to do. Everything happened so fast. She never expected anything like this. She felt weak and embarrassed. She wanted Jack to kiss her again but not here. Not in a place filled with people.

"You have embarrassed me!" She said in an angry quivering voice. "What are people going to say, Jack?"

"Now, when did Jennie Wade ever care about what the kind folks of Gettysburg thought about anything?" Jack chuckled. "Besides, look around, no one is even looking. No one." He continued laughing.

"Well, I don't care, Jack Skelly, what people are looking at. I just don't like to be kissed in public, in front of God and everyone." Jennie forcefully pushed him away and stepped back. "And, I don't really know your intentions with me, now do I?"

"Intentions. What do you mean by questioning my intentions?" By now Jack was getting a little frustrated and red in the face.

"My intentions have always been honorable by you," Jack proclaimed. "Always!"

Jennie, still taken back by the kiss, was speechless.

"I am sorry Jennie if I have offended your honor. You can be well assured I did not mean the offense." Jack paused for a moment, "It's just that I have been doing a lot of thinking about you and me and over this past winter and…"

"Well, this is not the place to be discussing such things, Jack," Jennie interrupted.

"You are right, Jennie. Yes, you are right," Jack said as he picked up his haversack. "Dan should be here any time and we can drop you off if you wish."

To her immense satisfaction Jennie just barely nodded her head in acceptance to this offer. "Georgia is with me tonight, Jack," she said in a matter-of-fact voice. "I asked her to walk up to the station with me."

"That's fine Jennie. Your sister is always welcome," he said as they walked side-by-side over to where Georgia was sitting on the bench.

"Miss Georgia," Jack said in a cautious voice. "It is nice to see you and Miss Jennie here greeting the troops. It is also nice to see friendly faces."

Georgia nodded. "It is good you are well Jack Skelly," Georgia said in a kind voice.

With a broad smile Jack looked at Jennie and then back to Georgia. "It appears that I have caused an embarrassing situation for your sister this evening," Jack said in an apologetic voice, looking right at Jennie.

"I am quite sure, Mr. Skelly, knowing my sister like I do, the embarrassment was about half of what you took it to be," Georgia chuckled, looking at Jennie standing there still caught up in the kiss. Jack smiled. "Dan and I will be taking you both home. You shouldn't be walking like that anyway Miss Georgia."

"Why, I am doing just fine Jack. We both thank you for your hospitality in taking us home, don't we Jennie," Georgia jested to Jennie.

Before Jennie could respond, Jack's brother Dan walked up to Jack and the sisters standing in front of the bench. He grabbed Jack and gave him a long bear hug. "Jack, it is good to see you. Everyone is excited and waiting at home for your arrival. I was not aware you were going to have such a gathering for your arrival," he said looking at the two sisters.

Fortunately for Jack, Dan brought their father's family carriage, which could seat four persons if Jack held his haversack. As they traveled through the town, both women were quiet. Dan made up for the silence by trying to get Jack to talk about what was going on in the war. All of Jack's answers to his brother were short and to the point. There was too much on his mind this evening, and Jennie was foremost in his thoughts. Jennie was sitting behind him in the carriage, and all he really wanted to do was turn around and share the many emotions on his mind about her.

Dan, wanting to give his brother and Jennie more time together, dropped off Georgia first, even though they had passed Breckenridge Street. Dan was aware of his brother's feelings about Jennie and he was also aware of Jennie's mother's feelings about their family. He knew it would be a rough week for both of them.

As the carriage turned onto Breckenridge Street, Jennie still had said very little. Jack would turn around and ask her a few questions about her family but other than small talk, not much was exchanged. As the carriage pulled up to Jennie's house, Jack turned around and broke the silence by asking if Jennie would like to meet tomorrow.

"Thanks for coming to the station tonight. You and Georgia have been so kind to my brother and me. You know, I am aware of how your mother feels about my family, so I know it was an effort on your part to welcome me home."

Jennie hesitated for a few moments and then said in a low whisper, "You are most welcome Jack. I have missed you!"

"May I call on you tomorrow, say around one o'clock?"

"Yes," Jennie said without any hesitation. "One o'clock would be just fine."

The moon, full and bright, illuminated the emotions of the moment in Jennie's face. She had so much to say, but this was not the time or place to share her unending love for this man. The week that loomed before them would be filled with solitary moments to exchange feelings and longings built up over the past six months.

Standing quietly by the door, Jennie prayed to God there would not be any lost moments over the next few days. She waited until the buggy started down the street then entered the house. She leaned up against the door for a few moments and took a deep breath. The house was dark and uninviting. She lit a candle, and the light filled the room with a soft glow. Everyone was in bed except her mother. She knew that her mother was probably in her room listening for Jennie's return, and would have something to say about it in the morning.

For now, she pushed those thoughts out of her mind. She would fall asleep tonight with only the wonderful thoughts of Jack's warm lips and his body pressed against hers. Again, she longed to be in his arms, wrapped in the blanket of his strength.

Upstairs Jennie could hear the wood floors squeaking in her mother's room.

"There will be the devil to pay in the morning, but, not tonight," she affirmed in a strong voice. "Tonight will be a night of wonderful dreams; dreams of things to come and a bright future. A future with Jack Skelly as we plan our life together during this wonderful week.

3
The Twin Springs
April 15, 1863

Jennie Wade was nervous. "I just don't know where my mind was last night," she said in an exasperated voice. "I should have told Jack that I would meet him somewhere else rather than here at the house. Then again, that would not have sounded proper," she theorized out loud.

Nervously Jennie looked at the kitchen clock, and then glanced out the window into the narrow alley alongside the house where she knew Jack would be coming from. It had been the tenth time in the last hour Jennie had checked the clock.

"I sure pray Jack will make it here before Mother comes this afternoon." Mrs. Wade had walked to the open market on the town diamond. For almost one hour now Jennie had paced back and forth from the kitchen to the parlor and then back into the kitchen. Harry was running in and out of the house taunting and badgering her in ways that only an eight-year-old brother could. Once he even threatened to tell their mother if Jennie did not take him to the store for penny candy. The one thing Jennie did not want to take place was a confrontation with her mother in front of Jack, and she agreed to Harry's terms.

At 1:15, a knock sounded on the door. Harry darted across the room, but Jennie managed to intercept him. "Harry Wade, where on earth do you think you are going?" she hissed, pulling him down to the floor by his pant straps. She then slapped him on his behind and pushed him out the side kitchen door.

"You wait, Jennie until Mother gets back. You are going to be in big trouble for having Jack here in the house," Harry hollered as he ran from the house.

Jennie quickly gathered herself together and opened the door. "Miss Jennie, how are you this fine day?" Jack said in a slow and pleasant voice, with his perfect white teeth gleaming through his broad smile. All her fears regarding her mother and her frustration with Harry melted away when she heard his voice.

"Why, I am doing just fine, thank you Jack," she said as she placed the last strands of her hair back into position. Jennie stood there as if paralyzed but moved slightly to let Jack in.

"Well, may I come in, or are we going to stand here and look at one another for the rest of the afternoon?" Jack questioned in an amused voice.

Embarrassed, Jennie let him in, despite thoughts of her mother walking up the steps of the house to discover them standing there. "Wait here by the door and I will gather my shawl, and the food basket," Jennie said in a concerned voice.

"Jennie, please let me help," Jack announced as he began to follow her into the parlor.

"No," Jennie said bluntly as she pushed him back into the doorway. "I will be back in a few moments. Please just stay right here."

As she entered the parlor, Harry, who was hiding behind the door, jumped out and startled Jennie. "Thought you were going to get away with this didn't you. Well, Mother is on her way back to the house and will be here in only a few minutes," he mocked.

"Harry Wade!" Jennie said in an angry voice. "You are a low-down sneaking varmint. Just wait until I get home tonight. You just wait.

Grabbing her shawl and basket, Jennie pushed Jack out onto the porch, and then down the steps onto the street. "Let's go, quickly!" Jennie exhorted as she grabbed his hand and led him away.

"What is this all about?" Jack said in a confused manner as they made their way to the waiting buggy. "Can I help in any way?"

"'Twas nothing. Just a little family misunderstanding, nothing more. You know how brothers can be."

"I sure do know how brothers can carry on, and such." Jack said shaking his head. "So, let's get out of here before that little monster comes back to get us both."

In a few minutes they were in the buggy turning off of Breckenridge Street south onto Baltimore Pike. The afternoon was perfect, with the temperature around 75 degrees. The sky was a clear blue except for a few fluffy clouds. The afternoon was turning out exactly how Jennie had envisioned. She realized this was the first time in six months she and Jack had been alone together. Her fear and anxiety melted away. For months, she had dreamt about this moment with Jack, thinking it was never to belong to her.

"Jennie, if you need someone to talk to, you know about the situation with your mother and all...well I just want you to know I will listen." Jack paused for a few moments to give Jennie time to answer.

"I know Jack. But, today I want to talk about us. I need to know many things. We just don't know how much time we will have together this week." Jack nodded his head in agreement as he cracked the whip, and the buggy took off at a fast pace down the street.

"Oh, by the way, I have decided I like the mustache you have grown since you have been away. It makes you look older," she disclosed with a smile.

"Well, I am just tickled to death that you approve. I must have spent long nights in my tent worrying whether or not Jennie Wade of Gettysburg would like it," Jack retorted with a chuckle.

"Be serious, Jack," Jennie exclaimed as she punched him lightly in the arm.

"No, I am serious. Yes, I am. I was a little concerned about the reaction of the folks back home here," Jack said laughing."

"You're impossible, Jack Skelly. I just don't know what I am going to do with you, but I do like your mustache," she said as she moved her body closer to him.

"Have you ever been over to the twin springs just south at the base of Culp's Hill on the farm of Abraham Spangler? I believe you know old Spangler, don't you?" Before Jennie could answer Jack continued, "Wesley Culp, along with my brothers and I, played there in our youth. Close to the twin springs is Rock Creek, which was our favorite swimming hole.

It would be a great place for us to go and spend the afternoon. That is, if it is all right with you?"

"That would be just fine, Jack. Spangler's spring has long been a landmark in the Gettysburg area, as you know." Jennie paused for a moment reflecting on her days there as a young girl when her family was together.

"Jack, do you know the story of how the springs were discovered?" Jennie questioned.

"No, I don't believe I know the story. That would be interesting to hear. Do you know the whole story?"

"Yes. My father told me about the springs when I was a little girl. You know the Henry Stahle family I believe. Well, Henry and some of his family were picnicking nearby and needed some water. On his way to Rock Creek, Henry saw some wet leaves in a low area surrounded by walnut trees, and when he stirred them with a stick, water bubbled forth.

"Stahle later secured permission from the farm's owner, Mr. Spangler, to clear out the spring and in doing so found another one and walled them both up. Well, from then on the springs provided water for a public picnic ground," Jennie pause for a moment making sure Jack was following.

"Very interesting Jennie. I guess I never knew the complete story. It's funny how things get started, isn't it?"

"Yes, it is Jack. Sometimes it's a miracle; like life itself. I remember the last time I was at twin springs. The springs were in the middle of a beautiful green field surrounded with tall trees, the tallest trees that I had ever had seen. I remember, also, that father chased Georgia and me around one of those trees. It was a good time. We were a family and it was wonderful. Then father up and went away and things were different at home. Mother has never been the same, you know. Our entire world changed, forever."

"Jennie, tell me about your father. I know only what the gossip has been over the years, and what my mother has told us," Jack said as he looked intently at Jennie.

"I haven't spoken of the abandonment to anyone, not even some of my closest friends. But, I guess you have a right to know the real secret of our family. Everyone in Gettysburg knows a little about the story, but not the complete one," she said, looking back at Jack and placing her arm through his.

"Thirteen years ago in 1850, father was convicted of larceny and sentenced to two years of solitary confinement at the Eastern Penitentiary."

Jack pulled back on the reins and the horse stopped abruptly, almost throwing them both forwards over the buggy. With a startled look he jerked his head up and over at Jennie. "That, I didn't know. We always thought he was just plain crazy," he acknowledged in an amazed voice.

"No, not at first. Father's conviction had something to do with picking up $300, which had fallen out of Samuel Durboraw's pocket while he was engaged in local town business. Rather than returning the money, as he should have, Father went off to Maryland and tried to make a flourish there. Are you still listening?"

"Yes, just trying to understand all of this," Jack said shaking his head.

"Well, unfortunately for Father, Mr. Durboraw and the town constable, Mr. Weaver, followed him to Maryland, and arrested him on the spot." Jennie paused for a moment looking for a reaction from Jack.

"I believe what really hurt the most was what happened after father was released from the penitentiary. Mother petitioned the Adams County Court to have father declared mentally insane. Father was turned over to the Adams County Alms House as mentally incompetent.

Father was never the same after that. None of us were." Once again Jennie paused, and looking over at Jack tried to see in his face his true reaction to her revealed secret.

"It's funny how things work out for us in life," Jack said trying to give Jennie support. "I guess I knew some of the story, but not the complete picture of what really happened to your father. A dirty shame. That's what it is, a dirty shame."

"I have never forgiven Mother for committing dad to the court. It branded the family as having not only a thief for a father, but a lunatic as well. The family never talks about any of this but...."

"You don't have to say any more, Jennie," Jack interrupted as he leaned over and cupped his hand over hers. "This is still very painful to you and quite sensitive. Why don't we talk about something else?"

"Ok, let's head to the twin springs," Jennie announced in a bold voice, holding on to the rim of the buggy.

The buggy took off on a wild run down Baltimore Pike. Dust from the road began to rise and circle around the couple, and in a few minutes they turned off of Baltimore Pike onto Spangler's Lane. They followed the lane for about a quarter of a mile as the dust continued to swirl around them. As the buggy came to an abrupt stop, the dust encompassed Jennie and Jack, covering them both in a light gray dust. Jennie began to sneeze as she wiped dust off of her shoulders, and arms.

"How did you like that ride?" Jack said laughing.

"I don't believe I have ever gone that fast before," she affirmed brushing the dust off her light green dress. "And, I don't ever intend to again," Jennie chirped as she climbed down from the buggy and began walking toward the springs at a fast pace. Jack picked up the food basket and ran after her down the grassy path paralleled on both sides by dark green spear grass

"You sure are fast when you want to be," he said out of breath. "You can plumb tire a man out now. Yes, you could."

Jennie continued walking down into the shallow valley where the two springs gurgled, surrounded by the tall dark walnut trees she had remembered from her youth. Jack followed behind trying to keep up with her fast pace. Outdistancing Jack, Jennie arrived first at the springs of cold clear water and splashed some in her face. The cool water felt good to her, refreshing her spirit and body as she splashed more on her neck and arms. Reaching into her dress pocket she brought out a handkerchief to wipe her face and neck.

"Let me help you; after all it was my driving that covered us in dust," Jack said as he removed the handkerchief from her hand and softly began to caress her face. Jennie trembled and turned her face away from him. He moved closer. Startled, Jennie moved further away from him.

"There's no one around now, Jennie," Jack whispered softly in her ear. She moved away again, only this time as she moved back, Jennie tripped over a limb and landed on her back in the tall spear grass. Laughing, Jack threw himself into the lush grass next to Jennie, and then rolled over onto his back.

For a few moments the two just lay there on their backs looking up at the spreading walnut trees, whose long limbs were covered with fresh yellowish green leaves. In-between the leaf-covered limbs a clear blue sky formed a perfect background. The leaves were gently moving in the soft breeze. Jack was sure he could hear Jennie's heart beating as she lay there beside him.

"Every thing around us is dancing. It's like life itself, Jack. Life is a wonderful dance," Jennie proclaimed.

"It sure would be nice if this day could last forever, just lying around in the tall grass looking up at the trees," Jack murmured softly to himself.

"It can, Jack, all of this can last forever in your mind, your thoughts. No one can ever take this afternoon from you and I."

Jack thought for a moment, "Well, I guess I have seen too much of death and young men dying to believe any of that today. I want to, but I just can't. Maybe someday I can believe," he said, looking intently into the sky.

He turned over onto his side and began caressing Jennie's hair. "I do know one thing that will last forever," Jack whispered into Jennie's ear smiling.

"What is that, Jack?"

"I love you. I have always loved you. There was never a time, not even back in school, that I cannot remember loving you."

Jennie was dumbfounded. She was totally taken by surprise and was speechless. She did not know what to say or even how to say it. The words she wanted to hear the most in this life had just been spoken to her and now she could not reply. Tears welled up in her eyes, and her heart was pounding so hard it felt as if it were going to jump right out of her chest. After a few moments Jennie regained her composure and looked into Jack's eyes for a reaction.

"I have always loved you too, Jack. But I never believed you felt the same for me. There was never any indication in any of your letters of your love or of your affection," she lamented in a voice filled with pain.

"Never once did you speak of love. I had no idea how you felt toward me. I had no idea what to expect at the train station yesterday. The whole day was spent in anguish and despair, not knowing how you were going to react to my presence Jack! There was nothing, nothing, and…"

"Jennie…"

"Let me finish, Jack Skelly. And I was left in the dark for six months. Do you know about all of the nights I cried myself to sleep after reading your cold indifferent letters? Do you know the pain of not knowing if you were dead or wounded? Weeks would go by without any communication from you at all. And, then, when I did receive a letter from you I was always afraid Mother would intercept the letter and destroy it. I hid the letters in the mattress of my bed so no one would ever find and read them," Jennie disclosed between sobs. Jack could no longer look into her eyes and began looking down into the grass. Jennie was speaking of things Jack did not want to hear.

"Jennie, I know, but..."

"Let me finish! Yes, Jack, I do love you too, and I always have and always will, forever, and nothing can ever change that, nothing. Do you understand how I have felt?" With her pent-up emotions and thoughts now shared and completed, Jennie bent down and kissed his cheek. Then again softly, as Jack's lips moved up to hers and they tenderly kissed and for a moment, a brief moment, the world stopped, as two souls were now united into one; one heartbeat, one breath, and one soul, for all of eternity.

Jack sat up bringing his knees to his chest, trying to hold back a flood of tears that came when he realized all of the sorrow and hurt he had caused Jennie over the last six months.

"I will make it up to you. I will," Jack vowed in a strong voice. "If it takes the rest of my life I will always let you know how much I love and care for you. I promise. I wanted to tell you a thousand times over of my love for you in every letter I wrote, but I could never reach down deep inside of me and bring those words to the surface. I just did not know how to say I love you," Jack divulged, looking to Jennie for forgiveness.

"I believe you will Jack Skelly. And I will always hold you to your word," Jennie avowed with a smile. "Maybe now is the right time for us to pledge our eternal love one to one another."

"Yes, I agree. A pledge, a covenant to each other would be wonderful," Jack, affirmed.

Jennie placed both of her hands in his and looking into his eyes began her pledge, her covenant of unending love. "I, Jennie Wade, pledge my unending love to Jack Skelly, to keep myself for him and him alone, for always. I swear this before our Eternal God of all creation."

Now it was Jack's turn. His words were slower, emerging from deep within his heart. "I, Jack Skelly, do pledge my eternal affection and love to the most wonderful woman I have ever known, so help me God." They sealed their vows with a long, lingering kiss.

"If I can secure a furlough in October, let's become engaged, or even married?" Jack said with a smile.

"That is just wonderful Jack." In her heart Jennie hoped that by the end of October they would become one.

Pulling a small book out of the basket she placed it on her lap. Jack stretched out alongside of her. "This is my favorite book, Jack, and if you don't mind, I would like to share some of my personal selections with you?"

Before Jack could protest, Jennie began reading, "'there was a time, when meadow, grove, and stream, the earth, and every common sight to me did seem appareled in celestial light.'"

Jack listened as her words pierced the silence of the surrounding woods. Outside of Jennie's voice, all that could be heard were the bubbling springs and occasional birds. Jennie continued, "'the glory and the freshness of a dream, it is not now as it hath been of yore: turn wheresoe'er I may, by night or day, the things which I have seen, I now can see no more.'" Jack thought her voice was the most heavenly sound he had ever heard and believed he could listen to her read every day of his life.

"'The Rainbow comes and goes, and lovely is the rose: the moon doth with delight look round her when the heavens are bare: Waters on a starry night are beautiful and fair: the sunshine is a glorious birth: But yet I know, where're I go, that there hath past away a glory from the earth.'" She paused and looked down, smiling, at Jack.

"'But there's a tree, of many one, a single field which I have looked upon, both of them speak of something that is gone: The pansy at my feet, doth the same tale repeat: Whither is fled the visionary gleam? Where is it now, the glory and the dream?'"

A hush fell over babbling springs, and in the distance over at Rock Creek the solitary sound of a whippoorwill in the trees could be heard. Jennie paused for a moment looking at Jack and then said, "This was written by William Wordsworth, and next to the Holy Bible it is one of my favorite books of poetry to read. It's called 'Intimations of Immortality.' I wanted to share a few of the lines with you today."

"I like it. I didn't think I would, but I do," Jack said looking deep into Jennie's eyes. "Then again anything you read out loud sounds good to me."

"And, this is my favorite verse of this work. Would you like to hear it?"

"Yes, I would, I really enjoy listening to you read, Jennie."

"'Though nothing can bring back the hour of splendor in the grass: we will grieve not, rather find strength in what remains behind.' That's how I feel about us. I will always feel close to you no matter what happens, do you understand, Jack? No matter what happens," she said softly, trying to control her tears.

"That was mighty fine Jennie, mighty fine indeed," he said as he rolled back over on his stomach, contemplating the words of Wordsworth.

There was a time; Jack thought about those words for a few moments, and then said to Jennie, "This is our time today, isn't it Jennie? Today is our time?"

"Yes Jack. This moment is our time, and we must make use of every minute we have together this week. Because we do not know how much time God will grant us," Jennie said as she lay back into the grass, exposing the fullness of her body to the open sky and trees. She turned and looked intently into Jack's face, studying the details. Jack said nothing as he memorized her face and hair.

He began moving his head closer to hers. Jennie closed her eyes, not wanting to look into his, knowing they were hungry for her. Slowly he worked his hand through her hair caressing it gently as Jennie's body began to stir. He then moved his fingers down to her lips and began brushing them softly across her mouth. She wanted to surrender totally to him but that would be a betrayal of her moral upbringing. A betrayal of her God.

Jack now moved his fingers from her lips to her neck and shoulder. Her body began to tingle and ache with his every caress. He then began kissing her neck, just under her ears, as the feelings of passion surged through her body like a lighting bolt. She reached out and placed his hand on her cheek as they kissed gently. Jack rolled over on his back and once again looked up at the canopy of trees, his mind filled with thoughts of passion, love, and war. "Right now, I am thinking that I don't want to go back to the war. In fact, I would rather stay here for the rest of my life."

"What are you saying, Jack?" Jennie said in a questioning voice.

"I don't want this day to ever end here at the twin springs," he said in a voice filled with certainty. "Sometimes, I don't think I will make it through this here war, Jennie. I just don't know."

"Stop that kind of talk, right now. Do you hear me Jack Skelly? You stop it right now. We are all going to make it through this war, and when you return, well, we can get married," Jennie announced.

"Get married! What makes you think I want to get married," Jack uttered, laughing. "You must think I am in love with you enough to marry you? Maybe I am, then again, maybe I'm not," Jack said trying not to laugh.

"Well, Mr. Skelly, it seems to me that just a few minutes ago you gave me your pledge of love. Now is that true, or is it not true?" she questioned. He stood up taking Jennie by the hands and pulling her up with him before answering her.

"You know it is true. And yes we can get married when I return this fall from Virginia. I should be home by October. We will get married in October! October is a good month to get married in," he announced. "Now, let's have some of that chicken you prepared and then go for a walk."

At Rock Creek, they skipped stones across to the other side. Then they waded in the cool water, trying to walk on the slippery moss-covered rocks in the creek bottom. Jack had to hold Jennie's hand or she would have slipped in several times over. They sat down along the bank of the creek where each was locked in their own thoughts, mesmerized by the babbling water.

The lazy afternoon drifted away as the day became a distant memory in their souls. It would be a day that neither would ever forget, a day to cling to with one mind, one soul, and one heart. As they left Spangler's Lane Jennie turned and glanced one more time at the twin springs before they entered the thick woods that surrounded the area.

Jennie slowly turned and looked intently into Jacks eyes."

"Life is full of surprises, and today has been one of those wonderful surprises," Jennie whispered to Jack as she slid her arm through his, and laid her head on his shoulder.

"Memories, Jack. Memories that will be savored in the winters to come. Savored in all their fullness, their glory, their passion, and their wonderment. Life is truly a wonderful dance."

"Yes, Jennie. Life is a wonderful dance."

4
The She Rebel
April 15, 1863

As Jack drove the buggy down the short, dusty lane leading to his home off of Baltimore Street, he noticed his father and brothers, Dan and John, on the front porch talking to John Burns. "I wonder what that old buzzard wants," Jack questioned. "I just hope the old fart isn't running for town constable again. The only time he comes around here is when he needs a few more votes," he said, shaking his head.

"Never did like the old man. He just loves spreading gossip, and at the same time, looking for fresh meat. He is a nosy old grouch, and a distempered one at that," Jack muttered to himself under his breath.

John Burns had settled in Gettysburg in the early 1830s, and for a time worked as a cobbler, and then took to drinking too much. For about three years, he was even labeled the town drunk. However, by 1840, he had reformed and had become a new creature, or so he claimed. In 1853, he was appointed constable of Gettysburg, a position that he held off and on until 1863. He had little use for Copperheads (pro-Southern folks from the North), which to him were the lowest of all forms of life. Burns had a desire to help preserve the Union by joining the army in 1862. But at 70 years old, he was turned down. This, coupled with his town drunk image, made him a bitter old man.

Jumping down from the buggy, Jack led the mare over to the shed and unhitched her as they disappeared into the shed. Looking out the small, dirty window, Jack could see Old Man Burns walking down the lane for home.

"Good riddance! He's nothing but bad news looking for a place to happen," he announced to his mare as he closed and latched the stall door. "Never did like the cantankerous old drunk," he muttered to himself. Leaving the shed, Jack turned, closed the old leather-hinged door, and noticed Dan running toward him at a gallop.

"What did that old fart want?" Jack questioned in an exasperated voice.

"The old coot wanted to know iff'n you brought any news of the Reb whereabouts," Dan blared in-between breaths. "He swears on a stack of Bibles the Rebs are going to invade the North, possibly our state." Jack wrapped his arm around Dan's shoulders as they walked. "Well, I reckon he might be right. Thing is, those Rebs will have to get by our series of forts we have in place all up and down the Shenandoah Valley."

"You know, Jack, he told us he is going to put together some kind of emergency force to defend the country against any invasion of the Rebs. I think he is real serious about this," Dan proclaimed. Jack remained silent as he lit his pipe and enjoyed a few strong puffs.

"I heard tell Burns was rejected when he tried to join a local army volunteer unit, yes I did." He paused and took another puff on his pipe. "Because of his age, we reckon. The old coot was probably around when George Washington organized the first army," he said laughing. "As I see it, little brother, iff'n the Rebs get this far up north with their army, ain't no volunteer army of John Burns going to be able to stop them. Now, you can take that to the bank, little brother." Jack paused and cleaned out his pipe by tapping it on the porch railing.

"The old fart may be crazy, but he is on target about one important thing, little brother. The Rebs are on the move and have been for a few weeks, and rumor is they are heading somewhere into the north. It won't be long until we all know where they are going to show up."

Dan's jaw dropped as he shook his head in disbelief. "Can't be Jack. Those Rebs would never think of invading the north, now would they?" Dan said in a concerned voice.

"Right now, at this very moment, we believe the Rebs are gathering at the Culpeper Courthouse area and are using the mountains to shield the army's movements. No mistake about it brother, the Rebs are coming north, and soon," Jack advised as he relit his pipe. "A victory on Northern soil could possibly bring England in on the side of the Rebs. Now that would be a fine howdy-do now wouldn't it, Dan?"

"But, do you think the Rebs are heading toward Gettysburg, toward our town, Jack?" Dan said in a serious voice.

"Gettysburg? No, I don't think so Dan," Jack affirmed in a strong voice. "The Rebs don't even know Gettysburg exists." With that assurance, some of the worry left Dan's face, but not all.

"Come on little brother, you have nothing to worry about. All the Rebs want to do is draw the Blue Bellies out into the open for a good scrap. And if they win this scrap they will descend upon Washington like some kind of Biblical plague on Egypt, and catch Old Abe with his pants down."

Dan sat there on the porch listening to every word his older brother was sharing. "Now, I ain't no Bible prophet, brother, but I can tell you this…" He paused, thinking of the correct wording to say to Dan to show his concern. "In this upcoming scrap with the Rebs, we had better win or all of our gooses are going to be cooked real nice-like."

Dan sat there looking out across the yard weighing every word Jack had shared with him. Entering the kitchen, Jack saw his father stoking the cooking fire. When he opened the door, a back draft blew a thin layer of smoke across the kitchen.

"War talk, Jack?" his father questioned as he walked over to the window and opened it. "Seems to me that is all one hears around here now-a-days," he said in a sarcastic voice.

"Well father, it seems to me we are in the middle of a war now, and a big one at that." Jack responded. "You don't suppose that is the reason we hear so much about war, do you?" Both brothers looked at each other and began to smile. Their father turned and with a scowl on his face left the room for more wood.

"Wonder what is bothering Father tonight?" Jack questioned his brothers. Both Dan and John turned and looked at each other with expressions of an old coon that had just been treed.

"All right, brothers, let's have it. Was it something old man Burns said that upset

Father?" Jack studied both boys, who by now were looking intently at the kitchen floor.

"It was! Wasn't it? Come on, you might as well tell me," Jack exhorted. "I want to know what that old man said to you and Father, and I want to know right now!" Jack roared.

Both brothers knew Jack well enough to understand they had better answer him, or there would be heck to pay. They both stood there looking at one another, waiting for the other to say something so Dan figured he would break the standoff.

"Old Man Burns told us that your friend Miss Mary Virginia Wade...well, talk has it she is a 'She-Reb' with feelings toward the south and all," Dan said reluctantly.

"Hold on there a moment, Dan. You mean Old Man Burns called Miss Wade, my Jennie, a 'She-Reb', a 'Southern sympathizer'?" Both brothers looked at one another for a few moments and then both nodded their heads at the same time.

"Why, that..." Jack caught himself before saying an unchristian word in front of his younger brothers. "Jennie is no 'She-Reb', I can tell you that, and by the end of this day, Old Man Burns will also know it," Jack announced for all in the house to hear. "Dan, I need to borrow your horse for a few hours. And you can tell Father where I am off to," Jack said as he walked out the door.

Both brothers looked at one another and shook their heads. "There's going to be the devil to pay by the end of this day, there surely is," Dan uttered to John.

"Ain't that the truth? I hope Jack remembers that the old fart is still the town constable. We might have to go down to the town jail and fetch him out." Both brothers began laughing with that prospect in mind.

"What are you boys up to," their father asked as he entered the kitchen with their youngest sister, Elmira. "I need help with the firewood boys, and I need it now. Let's get going." With that statement both brothers jumped off the porch and ran toward the woodshed, trying to see who would win the race.

The Skelly family had been fortunate in that their father had a good-paying job and the children were well supported. The 10 children were taught from birth that everyone in the family contributes by pulling their own weight, not only at home but also in the business.

Johnston Hastings Skelly, Jack's father, married Elizabeth Ann Finnefrock on June 21, 1837, and they lived their entire married life in Gettysburg. Johnston was the owner of the dry goods merchandise store in the Fahnestock building across Middle Street from the courthouse. The building was unique in that there was an observatory on top of the structure. The children of Gettysburg like to sneak into the store and climb the steps up to the "castle tower," and play "Knights Of Old." Jack, along with his close friends Wesley and William Culp, would spend hours playing in the observatory.

The Skelly family was known throughout Gettysburg as a close and hard-working family. No one in Gettysburg questioned the Skelly patriotism and loyalty to the Union. Everyone knew they would have to face Johnston Skelly himself if they questioned the cause of preserving the Union. Gettysburg had a few southern sympatherizers known as "Copperheads," and Johnston knew every one of them and where they lived.

Both Jack and his brother Charles were members of Company F, 87th Pennsylvania Volunteer Infantry. Jack was the first to enlist from his family. Charles wanted to enlist but their mother protested, stating he was too young. Even Johnston himself had enlisted, wanting to help where he would be needed. The family had been very fortunate that no one had been harmed; however, with each passing day, the family knew it would be only a matter of time.

Just as the family finished their late evening dinner, Jack was observed riding down the drive. Dan, Annie, and Elmira ran out to meet their brother before Jack had an opportunity to get off the horse.

"Tell us Jack," Annie shouted as they all ran up to meet their brother. "Tell us what happened, please."

Jack said nothing as he walked the horse into the shed and removed the saddle. Dan noticed that his brother had a little smirk on his face, as if trying not to laugh while he was removing the saddle.

"Come on Jack, tell us what happened. We won't tell Father. Promise," Dan pleaded as he helped close the gate and lock it.

"All I have to say is that old man Burns knows now that Miss Wade is not a 'She-Reb.'" As they reached the porch their father was waiting for them at the door. "Well, Jack, did you spare the life of our noble constable and valued citizen?" he questioned.

"I guess you could say that. I don't believe that old man will call Miss Wade any more names ever again," Jack scowled as he walked by his father and mother and disappeared into his room off the kitchen. As far as Jack was concerned, that matter with

Burns was done and over as he shut the door and threw himself onto the bed.

On the way back from the springs, Jennie had requested Jack drop her off at her sister's house on Baltimore Pike. Today was Georgia's first wedding anniversary, and Jennie wanted to be with her. It was also the wedding anniversary of their parents, but none of this was ever mentioned at home with the family.

Jennie was getting excited about the new arrival coming in a few weeks, and about becoming an aunt. Much of their time was spent in baby talk and preparation. Jennie loved children and wanted to have as many as God would grant her.

As they approached the house, Jennie noticed that the door was propped opened and Georgia was carrying in firewood. "George, what are earth are you doing carrying in all that wood?" Jennie questioned. "Please, let me carry in the wood. You should be resting," Jennie said in an exasperated voice.

"I can manage just fine, thank you. And, by the way, what are you doing here this evening?" I thought you were with Jack Skelly today! I was thinking about you both and praying that you two were working out some of the wrinkles in your relationship with your time together.

"I asked Jack to drop me here. I wanted to see how things were going with you today. Now, why don't you sit down here and relax and let me finish your chores," Jennie said as she moved her sister over to the table.

"Ok, Jennie, I will let you get away with this today. However, this is the first and last time I will sit down and watch my sister do my housework. As you work you must tell me every little detail about your afternoon with Jack," Georgia said in an inquisitive voice. "Everything!"

After bringing in the last of the wood, Jennie began to scrub the kitchen floors and share about her afternoon with Jack.

"The day was beyond what I ever dreamed of George. It began a little shaky with Jack being 15 minutes late. Knowing that mother could be home at any moment made me very nervous. But, by the grace of God, we were on the road before I had to deal with that situation," Jennie testified as she rinsed the washcloth out in the wooden bucket. "Oh George, the afternoon was wonderful, wonderful beyond belief," she paused and looked up at her sister. "I just did not know that Jack cared for me all that much. We both knew there had been nothing in his letters over the winter to indicate any affection toward me, but those letters misguided me with his real intentions."

"I don't want to pour water on your fire Jennie, but can you trust Jack with your emotions just like that," George questioned in a concerned voice. "You know he will be leaving at the end of this week, and who knows how long he will be gone this time. And will he write you? If I were you I would…"

"Well, you are not me and you were not there today so how can you understand how we feel?" Jennie interrupted. She continued, "Jack apologized about the letters, and explained why they were written that way. I accepted his apology and now I understand why he acted in such a manner."

Georgia sat there listening to her sister, wanting only the best for her and Jack. She paused for a moment to take a sip of hot coffee. "Jennie, I love you and want only the best. We both know how Mother feels, and if you and Jack can handle that stressful situation in your marriage you will both have a happy life together."

"I know you do, George. I must tell you something that happened at the springs this afternoon," she paused waiting for a response from Georgia. Jennie continued, "Jack and I pledged our love to each other today and we will become engaged this October when Jack comes home," Jennie shared with a smile.

"And, maybe we will even get married sometime during the month."

"Oh, Jennie, I am so happy for you both," Georgia said with tears flowing down her cheeks. "You deserve all the happiness that comes your way. It has been long time in coming," Georgia said as she removed her handkerchief and wiped her eyes. Jennie stood up and went over to her sister and gave her a strong hug. For a few moments both sisters stood there and hugged each other.

"Jennie, you should get married as soon as Jack comes home this fall if you can work out the details. You need to get out of that house and have a life of your own, just you and Jack. Jack comes from a good family and is well respected in Gettysburg. In spite of whatever mother feels, Jack would be a blessing to our family. Why don't you and Jack plan on coming over here tomorrow evening for dinner? I know Jack would want to. After all, he is a soldier, and soldiers, like their armies, move on their stomachs," Georgia said laughing.

5
The Rendezvous
April 16, 1863

Jennie could distinctly hear the clock in the kitchen downstairs strike three o'clock. She had been awake for most of the night, and with her mind going over all the events of yesterday she just could not get any sleep. She climbed out of her bed and went over to the old oak rocker that had belonged to her grandfather and began rocking. From where the rocker was located in her bedroom Jennie could look out the window and see the expanses of the ancient night sky that loomed before her.

For a few hours, Jennie sat there in the rocker and enjoyed the majestic splendor of the night sky. In the distance she could hear the call of a barn owl. The full moon was a bright pale yellow. Occasionally, a gray cloud would drift across the moon. The sky was endless, she thought. I wonder how far out it goes; maybe forever. She enjoyed looking into the infinite sky because she could easily lose herself in the eternal expanses. Her problems or joys, no matter how sad or happy, became lost and nonexistent compared to the night sky.

Tonight, Jennie's thoughts seemed different than even a few days ago. The events of the day seemed to have brought to Jennie calmness, purpose, and a rebirth. She was at peace, and her heart now had completeness.

"I wonder if Jack will give me a ring before he leaves Sunday?" Jennie whispered

"I would like to have a ring to wear until he comes home...yes, a ring would be nice...a ring would be very nice..." Sleep finally overcame her and her world went quiet.

She slept soundly until eight o'clock. The boys had been up since seven and had most of their chores completed by eight. Even her mother did not bother to call her for help in getting breakfast started, but let her sleep.

When Jennie awoke, she remembered to send Jack a message of the invitation for dinner at Georgia's home. She wanted to send Samuel over to the Skelly store on Middle Street early this morning, and she scurried to get dressed and downstairs before Samuel left. Jennie knew she would be busy throughout the day and would not know until this evening if Jack were going to show up on Georgia's doorstep for dinner.

Fortunately for Jennie, Samuel was still in the kitchen when Jennie came down, and the message could be delivered if Jennie could come up with 25 cents. At first Samuel wanted

50 cents, but Jennie threatened to walk the message over herself if he continued to ask for such a large amount of money. Samuel decided 25 cents was better than nothing at all, and headed up to the Skelly store with the message.

As Jennie walked up the stone steps off of Baltimore Pike to Georgia's house, she saw her sister out in the side yard pruning the fruit trees along the white picket fence.

"Going to have some mighty good peaches this summer," Georgia hollered across the yard when she saw Jennie coming up the steps.

"Sounds like some good peach pie awaits us by summer's end. We do love peach pie, now don't we, George?"

"Peach and apple, but by the looks of them there apple trees over yonder, we may be having peach pies only," she stated as they both picked up the freshly cut trimmings and placed them in a small pile by the water pump.

The afternoon slipped by, with Jennie helping Georgia prepare the chicken and gravy dinner and fresh baked apple cobbler. At five o'clock, both sisters could see Jack walking up the steps almost right on time.

The dinner was everything Jennie had thought it would be and more. Jennie had on the light blue dress she had been working on throughout the winter. She wanted Jack to be the first person to see her in the new dress and to feel his eyes wandering over her intently. Just thinking about this sent chills running through her body, giving her great pleasure. She wanted Jack to think of her as the most beautiful woman in the world.

Jack's reaction to Jennie, as he walked through the kitchen door, was the exact one she had been dreaming of all day.

"Wow! Miss Jennie you sure are looking mighty fine today. Yes, you certainly are. I don't believe you have ever looked as beautiful as you do today."

Jack noticed there was a rose color in Jennie's cheeks he had not seen before, even at the twin springs. There was something different about her, something special about the entire evening. Something Jack could not figure out, at least not at this moment. However, by the end of the night, he was sure this all would be clear to him.

Georgia was a wonderful hostess and made Jack feel right at home with her family. He loved the chicken and gravy, but praised over and over again the apple cobbler.

"The cobbler was better than Mother had ever fetched up for us at home. And now don't you go telling this out and about, or I will be in big trouble with Mother."

"You are very kind Jack, but I am of the mind your mother can out-cook me any time of the day," she proclaimed to all around the table. "Now, you take Jennie there," Georgia advised looking across the table toward her sister. "Well, she can also cook up a right good cobbler of any kind of fruit you so desire. Yes, she can."

"I am looking forward to that, Miss Georgia," Jack acknowledged with his broad smile as he made his way to the dry sink with his dishes. "In fact, I will be looking forward to many things when I return home this fall."

Blushing, Jennie followed Jack to the dry sink carrying Georgia's and her dishes.

"Now, what are you thinking about Mr. Skelly?" Georgia asked, as she glanced over to her smiling sister. Then Georgia looked at Jack who was sheepishly watching Jennie and trying to contain his broad smile.

"I am sorry, Miss Georgia, but we will need to be going as I have to get up very early to help Father, and I would like to spend a few minutes with Jennie alone. Now I don't mean to be rude and such but..."

"What Jack is really trying to say, George," Jennie declared interrupting, "is that we do not have much time to spend together this week and so tonight he would like to take me on a slow walk home so we can enjoy the rest of the evening together. Now, isn't that what you were a getting at, Jack?" Jennie affirmed.

"Yes, yes it was, Jennie. You do have a way with words. I thank you again Miss Georgia for such a wonderful evening."

The evening was cool as the couple slowly walked up to Evergreen Cemetery on East Cemetery Hill. The Cemetery was the community burial ground, (established in 1756) and located on the west side of the Pike; it's arched, brick gatehouse provided access from the Pike. The main cemetery grounds occupied the hill's west crest. The northwest slope was covered with orchard trees, fences and stonewalls that crisscrossed the slope of the hill.

The cemetery was rich in local history and contained the remains of many of the early prominent citizens of Gettysburg. The cemetery had been a favorite place of solitude for Jennie, and she spent many hours walking among the tombstones, reading the epitaphs and committing her favorites to memory.

The epitaph Jennie like above all others was about a husband and seven wives. She had memorized it years ago, and would often recite it to herself.

"Seven wives are buried with a fervent prayer, if we all should meet in heaven-won't there be lot of trouble there," Jennie would recite the verses aloud and then laugh.

For years Jennie wanted to bring Jack to the cemetery, but she never had an opportunity; now here they were walking through the large Gatehouse entrance off of the Baltimore Pike Road. Walking through the Gatehouse both saw the bold lettered sign at the same time and began laughing. The sign read, "Warning! The use of firearms is forbidden in the cemetery and violators will be prosecuted to the fullest extent of the law."

"Now, who would be so disrespectful as to discharge a firearm in this place, I ask you?" Jack questioned Jennie, while trying to maintain an appearance of respect.

"Jack Skelly, please show respect in this place," Jennie advised, but at the same time was having difficulty in controlling her own smile.

"You know Jack you are not even allowed in here after sunset, which is also the town law, but I still come here quite often in the evening and gather my thoughts. Mostly, over the past six months my thoughts have been of you, Jack." They both stopped walking just inside the gate and stood there gazing into each other's eyes.

"I was torn in what to do about us. Six months is a long time to go without any affirmation of love or affection from someone you know you love. And it hurt. You will never know how much I really missed you," Jennie whispered in a sad voice.

"You are right, I will never know about how much you have missed me. But I was thinking about you every day and almost every minute. I just did not know what to say or how to say what I felt were proper words to you," Jack answered in an anguished voice.

He bent over and gently kissed Jennie, holding her tight against his powerful chest. She pulled his body more tightly against hers, and felt his strength encompass her body. She wanted the moment to last forever; however. Sensing her body heat up with powerful urges, she pushed him back and away from her, then changed the subject.

"Oh, Jack, it's such a beautiful evening here in the cemetery. I could stay here forever.

"Jennie, now watch what you say," Jack cautioned in a loud whisper. "Don't forget where we are." They both looked around at the stark gray tombstones and began laughing.

Jack looked deeply into her eyes. Jennie was the vision of all that he had ever desired or could ever want. He knew after this week he would never be able to get enough of her. With every kiss, it became more difficult for him to leave on Sunday. All they had was the moment. Moments built upon other moments, creating memories that Jack would be able to recall in his mind later, in the heat of battle.

He kissed her again. Only this time with firmness that created a rush he had never experienced before. The kiss forced Jennie back against a tombstone and she felt its cold dampness against her back. She closed her eyes as he kissed her again in ways that a woman wants to be kissed.

"Jack," Jennie cautioned. "We have got to stop or I will be wanting you all the more. I know we have exchanged our vows, but we still are not married. Do you understand?"

"Yes, Jennie I do understand. Sometimes I think God will take you from me, because I do not deserve such a wonderful person as yourself."

Jennie became quiet as they continued to slowly walk through the cemetery looking at the various stone slabs. The night air was crisp and clear, and the evening sky was beginning to fill up with stars as bright as sparkling diamonds. In the background they could hear the spring tree frogs and crickets. The woods seemed to come alive all around them as they stood there on top of the hill, looking across the ancient skies.

Throughout the day, Jennie had been thinking about Jack's train that was to leave on Sunday. For some reason the idea of him leaving so soon had not reached her until this evening.

"Jack," Jennie said looking into his face but not his eyes. "About you leaving this Sunday..."

"Jennie," Jack exclaimed. "I thought we had both agreed at the springs you would not come to the station. We both know this is the best this way. Now, I will hear no more of it. Do you understand? No more talk of the train station."

Jennie knew she would never receive Jack's approval to be at the station when he left Sunday. She was also aware Jack Skelly had changed her life forever and nothing or no one would keep her from going to the train station this coming Sunday morning.

"Yes, Jack I understand, I will not be at the station when you leave Sunday," Jennie conceded, with her fingers crossed behind her back.

6
The Good-Bye
April 18, 1863

Jennie never remembered Gettysburg having so many people milling and walking about the streets. It felt to her as if the entire borough was out and about on this mild Friday afternoon.

Gettysburg was the county seat for Adams County, a borough that had grown to around 2,000 people. More important, the borough had the advantage of becoming a hub of a network of 12 major roads, which pointed in every direction. The roads, which radiated from the Town Square or diamond, as the citizens called it, passed through a rich agricultural county of well-tilled fields and large red barns. Hard working farmers of German and Dutch extraction built the farms years ago.

Gettysburg was founded in 1781 and named after John Gettys. In its 82-year history, Gettysburg had grown into a prosperous farm town with the distinction of having two colleges, Pennsylvania College and the Lutheran Seminary.

Jennie was quite aware of the town's history and growth from her early childhood.

She had been born in Gettysburg on May 21, 1843. Yet, it appeared to Jennie that the recent increase in the population of the town had taken a turn for the worse, with the increase in street traffic. On the other hand, she thought the increase in the population was good for the businesses such as Jack's family's store and other stores that lined the narrow streets of the town.

As Jennie continued walking through the crowded streets window-shopping, she could not make up her mind what to purchase for Jack as a going-away gift. Georgia had given her a few suggestions for the price range she could afford but so far nothing suited her. Time was running out, and in a few days Jack would be gone until October.

Walking down York Street toward the Town Square Jennie noticed a store she had walked past many times before but had never entered because of a lack of funds. Between what Georgia had given her and what Jennie had saved, there was enough money to buy Jack a nice blue calico shirt.

As Jennie was just about to enter the store she noticed a small group of soldiers walking at a fast pace in the direction of the train station. Following behind that group of soldiers were another four soldiers dressed in full gear.

Jennie, being inquisitive, and knowing the earliest train to leave with troops was Sunday morning, not Friday, stopped one of the soldiers to inquire what was taking place.

"Miss, all I can tell you is our company has been ordered out sooner than any of us desired. We leave tonight." The young soldier turned and continued walking with his fellow comrade in arms.

"Sir," Jennie called out to the young soldier, "Do you know a soldier by the name of Jack Skelly?" she questioned with a voice filled with concern.

"No, I do not, Miss. If he is in Gettysburg on leave you can almost bet that his company is moving out earlier too. I'm sorry," he shouted, "I'm sorry Miss," He tipped his forage cap and disappeared around the corner.

Surely Jack would have told her he was leaving on Friday instead of Sunday. Jack would have said something to me; I know he would have, she thought as she began walking to the station.

As she came closer to the station Jennie noticed groups of soldiers carrying large amounts of gear as if they were going to be away a long time. A wrenching heaviness took control of her body leaving her like a limp rag.

"If Jack was leaving tonight or tomorrow sometime," she muttered to herself in the confusion surrounding the station area "he would have told me. He should have said something." She began to walk away from the station as fast as her feet would take her.

"God would not do this. I know He would not do something like this to me. This is all a misunderstanding and after I talk with Jack's father everything will be all right," she moaned in-between sobs.

Jennie wiped her face with her apron, pinched her cheeks, and began walking to the Skelly store on Middle Street.

"If anyone knows what on earth is happening around here it would be Jack's family," she muttered to herself as she increased her walking pace. As the store came into view she noticed Jack's brother Dan sitting on the front porch working over a pickle barrel. When Jennie saw Dan she came to an abrupt stop. "I don't want Jack's family thinking I am an old busybody trying to stir up information and what-not. But, I have to know what is happening to Jack," Jennie anguished out loud to herself.

"Miss Wade, can I help you with something today?" Dan questioned as he slowly stood up and placed the lid onto the barrel.

Jennie was embarrassed and was sure that Dan could see that see has been crying and involuntarily brought her hand up to her cheeks.

"Uh...no! I thought maybe Jack was here at the store helping out," Jennie said with reservation.

"Last time I saw my brother was this morning. I thought he might come over to the store and give us a hand today." He paused as he ran his hand through his long hair.

"Maybe he is just making the rounds to see his friends before he leaves Sunday. I just don't know. If I see Jack I will make every effort to let him know you are looking for him," Dan avowed to her.

"Thank you Dan. If you find out where he is please let me know as soon as possible," Jennie admonished, fighting back the tears.

Because Dan was Jack's brother, talking to him gave her closeness to Jack that Jennie needed. She thought the conversation with Dan had helped her to feel better about whatever was going on with the army, and yet something inside her would not allow her complete peace about the situation.

As Jennie walked through the door Samuel handed her a sealed envelope containing a note and ran out the back door. She immediately recognized Jack's handwriting.

With trembling hands Jennie opened the envelope, unfolded the paper and began reading.

"My dearest Jennie, just a brief note to inform you that I will be leaving first thing Saturday morning with my company. I have no idea why we have to leave one day earlier but we do. Will meet you at the cemetery Gatehouse at eight o'clock. Love always, Jack"

Jennie's face was ashen white as she slid to the floor of the parlor. "Oh my God, it is true," she cried. "I can't believe God would allow this to happen. We only had a few moments together, that's all. A few moments," she moaned.

"What I am going to do?"

She gathered herself up from the floor and went up to her room and closed the door. After Samuel told their mother, who was out in the garden working, about the letter, she went to Jennie's bedroom and knocked on her door. Jennie refused to answer, so her mother opened the door and walked in.

"I don't really want to talk at this moment," Jennie said in-between sobs. "Maybe we can talk later."

Her mother walk over to the bed and sat down on the side chair. "Is there anything I can do for you? I know how you must feel and I..."

"No, there is nothing you can do for me! And, you don't know how I feel!" Jennie asserted, interrupting. "Jack means nothing to you. He is just another soldier going off to war. I may never see him again," she said crying. "Now, please leave me alone!"

"You're wrong, Jennie. I do care about you. I have always cared about my children. Do you think it was easy when your father left leaving a house full of mouths to feed and no money to buy food?" she said in a voice of anguish.

"Everything that I have done over the last few years has been for you children. Certainly not for me." Her mother paused and placed her hand on Jennie's shoulder.

"Now listen to me. If this is meant to be, everything will work out for you both. In the end, God will have his way." Jennie remained silent as her mother walked over to the door and disappeared into the hall. Jennie rolled over in the bed and went into a fitful sleep.

At 7:30, Jennie began her walk up to the Gatehouse on Cemetery Hill. Reaching the Gatehouse, Jennie noticed Jack was already there. He was leaning up against the brick structure with the most dejected face she had ever seen. His uniform had been cleaned and pressed, and even his leathers looked cleaned and oiled in the moonlight. He appeared to her as a handsome Knight making ready for war. But war was not what she wanted to talk about tonight.

As soon as Jack saw her walking toward the Gatehouse he began to shake his head, while trying not to show any emotion. He wanted to act strong for Jennie, stronger than any other time in his life. The last thing he wanted to do was to leave and go off to war. He was aware it could be a long separation before they could be together again.

Jennie felt cold and lifeless even as Jack wrapped his warm, strong arms around her shoulders. For a few moments, they both looked into each other's eyes, and said nothing. They were both aware nothing really needed to be said at this moment. They both knew a good-bye would be painful.

"I believe I have always known how this weekend would end," Jennie said, breaking the silence. "None of this seems fair, does it Jack?"

Jack did not answer. Instead, he held her closer to his body, feeling the beating of her heart, and the warmness of her soul touching his. He gently held her head and kissed her lips softly.

"Listen Jennie," Jack whispered in her ear. "We were both aware this could happen. In fact, I am a bit surprised it didn't happen sooner. You must understand what I am about to say. You must listen to me, please," he implored, holding back the tears forming around the corners of his eyes.

"I believe it is best if you did not come to the train station tomorrow morning, Jennie. It would be very difficult for both of us. You do understand, don't you?"

"No! No, I don't understand, I don't under-stand any of this!" Jennie sobbed as she broke away from Jack and ran into the cemetery.

Jack ran after Jennie and grabbed her arm, swinging her around into his arms. She wrapped herself around his body sobbing. Jack held her tight, trying to console her.

He kissed her with such a force that her breath was taken away. She wanted more. She brought her body closer to his, desiring to feel his strength envelop her entire body.

"You have not promised me yet that you will not come to the station. Will you promise me that?" Jack questioned her as he held on to her waist and pushed her out in front of him so he could see her face in the bright moon light.

Jennie said nothing as she turned her face away from his and stared into the darkness.

"Jennie, do you promise?" Jack questioned again, only this time in a much sterner voice.

"Yes Jack! I promise you I will not go to the station," Jennie muttered with her head looking down and her fingers crossed behind her back. In her mind there was never any doubt that she would not be there in the morning.

Jack drove Jennie back to their house on Breckenridge Street and walked her up the porch steps. Jack gave her a lingering kiss that Jennie felt as if it lasted forever.

"Now, don't forget to write me," Jennie said in-between kisses.

"I will write you a letter every week," Jack answered.

"Ok. You'd better or you will have to answer to me when you return."

Jennie held on to Jack as long as she could. The moment came however, when Jack had to leave and she knew she would have to let him go.

"Please Jennie, I have to go," he said as he gently pushed her away, turned and walked down the steps. Just before he climbed up into the buggy he turned and ran back up the steps and gave Jennie one last passionate lingering kiss. He then turned, climbed up into the buggy and drove away without ever looking back.

Jennie stood there watching him go, with tears running down both cheeks. Jack's departure was silent, as silent as the cooing of the night dove murmuring its own sweet cry, neither too soft nor too loud. Its wings cutting through the cold of the April night, moving in swirls, diving and swooping in miniature curls, showing, in its own way, pure love in flight. Jennie entered the house, went into the parlor laid down on the sofa and was asleep in minutes from pure exhaustion.

Jennie was awakened by the striking of the kitchen clock telling her it was seven o'clock. Still half asleep, she rolled back over and closed her eyes until her mother came into the parlor and woke her up again. After lying there a few moments, she quickly raised up. "Jack's train was leaving at eight o'clock, and it will take me at least 20 minutes to walk up to the station," she exclaimed in a loud voice.

She looked at the kitchen clock and saw that it was now 7:15. She would only have 15 minutes to spare and decided to forgo any cleaning up and left the house in the same dress she had slept in.

In the distance, she could hear the courthouse clock strike 7:30 and began to pick up her pace.

"Please God don't let his train leave until I get there. Please," Jennie prayed, as she ran.

Approaching the station, she could hear the steam from the train and the sound of the soldiers gathering and climbing into the boxcars with their various units. Her heart began beating faster as she entered the station door at a full run, ignoring the people gathered around. Her hair was undone and her dress, soiled with sweat and dirt made her quite a spectacle to the gathering crowd.

Entering the long ramp area, Jennie noticed the last group of soldiers boarding the boxcars. A few feet away a small band was playing "Kathleen Mavourneen." The crowd, all with somber and tear stained faces were gathering around the band as they played, waiting for the train to depart.

"What a sad song to be playing as these here soldiers leave," Jennie muttered to herself as she continued running along the ramp parallel to the train. She ran as fast as her legs would take her to the last two soldiers boarding the train. The last soldier in line was startled to see this little, disarrayed woman standing beside him with streaks of sweat running down her face and breathing hard.

"Can I help you Miss?" the soldier questioned not knowing what to expect.

Jennie acted as if she never heard him and continued looking up and down at the windows of the train cars. The soldier shrugged his shoulders and climbed aboard just as the door was beginning to close.

As the train whistle blew, the train slowly began to move with the steam coming from underneath the wheels. The steam began to encircle Jennie standing there looking up at the windows.

"Please God, let me see Jack one more time before he leaves," Jennie prayed to herself.

Jack had just boarded the train as Jennie ran through the gate. It was warm and stuffy inside the car, which smelled like old cigars and leather. He found a window seat and before placing his gear in the seat across from his, opened the window for fresh air.

After he was seated, Jack looked out the window at the gathered crowd below. Scanning the crowd he noticed a young girl standing on the ramp looking up at each window. Her hair was in disarray and her dress soiled. After watching her for a few moments he realized this woman was his Jennie.

"Jennie! Jennie!" Jack called out with excitement.

"What on earth are you doing here?" he questioned. "You promised me, Jennie. You made a promise!" Jack shouted above the roar of the train.

Before Jennie could answer Jack, the train began moving slowly, and she had no choice other than to begin walking alongside while looking up at Jack. Fighting back tears, she tried speaking over the increasing noise.

"You know, Jack, I would never make a promise like that without crossing my fingers behind my back," Jennie yelled. "Besides, even if I had made that promise without crossing my fingers, I still would have shown up."

Jack smiled, but it was a nervous smile.

The train picked up more momentum, and Jennie had to increase her pace as she continued looking at Jack in the window.

"Jennie, don't forget what we talked about at the springs. I meant every word," Jack yelled. He stuck his head out the window in order to be closer to Jennie.

Jennie ran up to the window and stretched out her hand to his, and for one brief moment they locked hands.

"Don't leave me Jack. It's not fair. Not like this. Not now. Not ever. I love you, don't forget, I will always love you no matter what happens," she cried.

"Jennie, I love you too. Wait for me, I will come back, I promise you. Remember, I will always love you no matter what happens," he shouted as their grip separated. Jennie watched in slow motion as their hands disconnected and the train picked up speed.

Jennie could no longer keep up the pace necessary to stay by Jack's window, and in horrified silence she watched the train disappear down the tracks like a silent vapor, cold, separating, as if forever.

She stood there oblivious to her surroundings with her hand still held up, reaching out to something that was no longer there. Too weary now to cry, and with numbness flowing through her body, she slowly turned and began walking through the thinning crowd.

As she walked, in her mind Wordsworth's words gave her the comfort she needed and she began to recite the words out loud.

"'What, though the radiance which was once so bright, be now forever taken from my sight. Though nothing can bring back the hour of splendor in the grass, of glory in the flower: we will grieve not, rather find strength in what remains behind,'" she whispered to herself.

Far down the track Jennie could hear the train whistle blowing, carrying her Jack and her strength away. In the distance the voice of a high tenor could be heard about the clatter of the train station. The singer was finishing the last verse of the song the band was playing; "It could be for years, or it could be forever."

7
The Gathering Storm
June 1863

In the months after Jack left, Jennie had said little. She stayed around her house, trying to keep busy except for the few times she visited Georgia. Her family, for the most part, left her alone in her sadness. Even her mother, who in the past would have made an occasional comment about the Skellys, never mentioned anything about Jack.

Jennie's days were spent quietly, and to some extent as they were before Jack came home on his furlough last April. The family's tailoring business was thriving, and the busy workload, for the first time since Jennie could remember, had become a blessing, not a curse. Their largest customers were W.T. King, and Johnston Skelly, both merchants in Gettysburg.

The one bright spot for Jennie these days was the coming birth of Georgia's baby, due sometime in late June just a few weeks away. For Jennie the coming birth was exciting and brought her a little happiness. She was praying Jack would be back in the autumn to share in the excitement and blessings of Georgia's new baby.

Autumn had always been her favorite time of the year. She loved how the rolling hills of Gettysburg would be covered with the splendor of brilliant colors. And this coming fall would be even more special to her when Jack returned and they resumed their marriage plans.

In the surrounding area outside of Gettysburg, rumors continued to abound, and with three weekly newspapers in Gettysburg the rumors of the Rebs coming to the area were constant. Every week since the last day of May, rumors increased as to what the Rebs were up to; and when and where they would appear.

Due to the numerous false alarms of invasions to the area, since early 1862, many of the residents of Gettysburg were confident that Lee's army would show up some place else.

For Jennie, the rumors made no difference to her. Her only thoughts were of the safe return of Jack Skelly and their marriage in October. Jennie was very proud of Jack and knew he would be playing an important role in keeping the Rebs out of Pennsylvania, and Gettysburg.

What Jennie was not aware of was that the Confederate rank and file was now at its zenith of military self-assurance. This led the South down the road to overconfidence with its military endeavors. However, just the same, the South was riding the crest of its military power, and nothing the Union threw in its path seemed to stop them.

In the North, Lincoln was desperately changing generals in search of the one general who would take a stand against Lee's Army of Northern Virginia and win. To some in Gettysburg, the future of the Grand Union seemed bleak and dark indeed; a darkness that covered the north all the way to Washington.

Every evening Jennie knelt by her bed to say her prayers for Jack's safe return to Gettysburg. However, since the last week in May, Jennie had also been praying that this darkness of a Reb invasion hovering over Gettysburg and the Union troops would leave, freeing up the citizens for better production and work. Jennie was keenly aware that the future of the Union and her Jack were all in the hands of God. But, even knowing this, she felt surrounded on many evenings during her prayer time by some foreboding presence that encompassed her. Little did Jennie realize that at the very moment of her evening prayers, less than 80 miles southwest of Gettysburg, this darkness was bearing down on Jack and his fellow soldiers.

Jennie's premonition of foreboding took the form of a Lieutenant General Richard S. Ewell, commander of Lee's Second Army Corps. Ewell would be a powerful force for the Federals to reckon with in mere hours.

The town of Winchester, Virginia, was a crossroads rail terminus of some 3,500 people. Winchester was located in the heavily wooded Northern Shenandoah Valley, and was surrounded by a paradise of natural beauty. Unfortunately, for the citizens of Winchester and Corporal Jack Skelly, the town was positioned directly in the path of Lee's invasion route into Pennsylvania. General Lee would not allow a Federal garrison at Winchester with 5,100 federal troops to remain behind his army as he continued marching north.

Covered by General Jenkin's cavalry brigade, General Ewell set out from the Culpeper, Virginia area on June 10, 1863 for the Shenandoah Valley, which was an open door into the north. General Ewell's orders and mission from General Lee were very clear and precise. He was to clean out the Shenandoah Valley and remove all federal garrisons scattered throughout the valley, thereby protecting the Army of Northern Virginia's flank.

For weeks, Union General Henry Halleck had been trying to get his commander at Winchester, Major General Robert Milroy, to move his troops from a very dangerous position and to regroup in a safer area. General Halleck suggested Milroy move his troops to the safety of Harper's Ferry some 30 miles to the northeast as soon as he could make the arrangements; before it was too late.

However, General Milroy insisted they could hold Winchester against any force the Rebs could bring against them. The soldiers under his command, including Jack Skelly, thought differently, and wanted their General to move to the safety of Harper's Ferry.

In the early morning fog of June 13, 1863, General Ewell of Lee's Second Corps began his attack on the federal detachment south of Winchester. After a brief but fierce skirmish, General Milroy ordered his troops to withdraw to the three forts north and west of Winchester. The next day, June 14, 1863, President Lincoln wired General Milroy to get to Harper's Ferry if at all possible. Lincoln believed that if General Milroy and his army stayed in Winchester, the army would be all but destroyed by the advancing Rebs. Unfortunately, it was too late.

With close to 23,000 officers and men in his three-division corps and Jenkin's cavalry, old "Baldy" Ewell moved fast and furious and attacked the three forts. In a move worthy of his predecessor, Stonewall Jackson, Ewell sent Major General Jubal Early moving through the dense woods around the west fortifications of the fort. After a brutal artillery duel, the Confederates charged at 6:30 in the evening with the Rebel yell piercing the cool air. The young Federal soldiers, many that had never heard the Rebel yell before, shook with fear. The soldiers could hear the frightful sound long before Hay's Brigade charged headlong into the west end of the fort destroying everything in its path. Early's division seized the breastworks after intense hand-to-hand fighting driving what remained of the Union forces into the main fort.

Around 10 p.m. General Milroy thought he was surrounded and decided on an immediate retreat from the main fort to Harper's Ferry. General Ewell had already predicted this move and sent General Johnson's fresh division to enjoy a good scrap with the blue bellies. The move to counter a Federal escape would turn into a surprise party for the boys in blue.

The Federal army was intercepted at a bridge, which spanned a deep railroad cut. Around 3:30 a.m., after a brief exchange of shots between the scouts and skirmishers, the Federals surprised General Johnson with an immediate frontal assault. The frontal charge in the dark was something the Federal army was not ever known to do. General Milroy was determined to break out of the trap and continued his thrust toward Harper's Ferry at any cost.

Jack had been placed in the second wave of Union soldiers who charged along the turnpike road in complete darkness. Alongside of Corporal Skelly were two close friends from Gettysburg, Sergeants William Ziegler and Billy Holtzworth. However, even with his friends close by his side, Jack felt insecure and disoriented as he ran through the darkness toward the unseen enemy. The terrible sounds of fighting engulfed the three friends as they remained close together.

"Jack! Jack! Are you there?" Sergeant Ziegler shouted as the command was given for double-time along the dirt road. The three friends tried to stay right along side of the road so as not too wander to far off and right into the Rebs.

"Yes, William. I am right behind you," Jack yelled above the roar of battle.

"Don't stop or I will run right into you with my bayonet."

"Yeah, and I am right alongside of Jack," Billy cried out.

"Now, you boys stay right behind me and don't get yourselves up and lost," William bellowed out. "And keep your heads low. Can't do much without a head now, can you?"

What the three friends did not know was about 100 yards in front of the Union advance a narrow bridge over the railroad cut was armed with a Reb cannon loaded with full canister.

With daylight approaching, Jack strained his eyes and could see the dark forms ahead; lined up on both sides of the road was what looked like the enemy and a cannon.

"Hey, Bill! William! Do you see what I see across the road ahead of us?" Jack shrieked.

"Yeah, we do!" Both Billy and William answered at the same time. "Maybe our commander will have us get off of this here dang road where we are all sitting ducks and cut across the field to the right and outflank them there Rebs," William shouted.

"Nope! Don't think so. Now, that would be too clever for the high command to do something like that," Jack answered. "Command will have us charge straight on into the cannon fire so there will be lots of casualties, and...." Just then a shell burst along side of the three friends, knocking them down to the ground with the concussion of the explosion.

"Somehow," Jack said, as he was lying flat on his face in the road, "we'd better stay down for a spell and rest. I have a feeling we are going to need all the rest we can get before the night is over."

No sooner had they been thrown down on the road, a rifle volley from the Rebs less than 50 yards away swept over their heads, killing four of the soldiers walking directly behind them. Jack could hear the lead minie balls whine just a few feet over his head.

"That was close," "William announced to the others. "That was real close! Good thing we were all laying down when that Reb volley was discharged or we would have all been kilt!"

The fighting raged over the next several hours as Milroy ordered charge after charge toward the bridge until the Confederates were nearly out of ammunition. Each time the Federals were within 20 yards of the bridge, the Rebs would fire grape and canister shot from the cannon positioned on the bridge.

In only a few minutes, the ground in front of the bridge was covered with dead and wounded Federal troops. Yet, in spite of the heavy losses by the Union troops, victory was only minutes away. The Confederates were out of ammunition!

As the sun came up, Walker's Unit joined Stewart's Brigade reinforcing the Reb strength at the bridge, and with more ammunition, laid down a heavy fire into the Union ranks. The Federal formations broke and the soldiers began to turn and run in all directions.

As Jack and his friends lay along the edge of the road, they could see the forms of men running pell-mell past and over them, many, throwing down their weapons as they ran. The Rebs then counter-attacked out of Carter's Woods and swept across the open field along the right flank of the Union troops, taking many prisoners in their path including the three friends from Gettysburg.

General Johnson's skillfully placed trap was successful even though General Milroy succeeded in escaping. The good General left behind over 4,000 prisoners of war, 443 casualties, 23 cannons, 300 well-stocked wagons, and a wounded Corporal Jack Skelly.

Jack was among the many prisoners who had been captured when the Federal lines broke in the Carter's Woods area. William Culp, the brother of Wesley Culp who went south before the war and joined a local unit, was the only one out of the friends from Gettysburg to escape along with the good General Milroy.

Jack, along with William Ziegler, Billy Holtzworth, and William Culp decided when they entered the war that there was no way they were going to spend time in a disease infested Southern prison camp. Prison would be a slow death and Jack would never see Jennie again.

From the moment Jack was captured, he immediately began looking for a way to escape and after about one hour as a prisoner of war an opportunity to escape opened up. One of the guards turned and walked over to another guard for some pipe tobacco and Jack, along with two other soldiers, saw their chance and began running toward a densely wooded hillside about 50 yards away.

As Jack ran, his tired, tormented muscles, stiff from the day's fighting would not let him keep up with the other two soldiers. However, after 20 yards of running his leg muscles began loosening up. Jack increased his speed and made every effort to catch up with the other two. He began running in great smooth strides, carrying his body across the grassy field toward the dark gray woods and freedom.

He could hear guns cracking behind him but dared not look back. Even as Jack felt the wind from the deadly lead pass by his head, he kept running for all he was worth. With his lungs about to burst, Jack approached the edge of the woods and could hear birds singing throughout the forest. "How can birds be singing in a world gone crazy like this?" he muttered to himself, with his lungs about to burst, "It is just a crazy, crazy world," he muttered again to himself.

Jack approached the edge of the woods at a full run. A great feeling of triumph filled his spirit as he increased, rather then slackened his speed in the last few yards. Jack could smell the dampness of rotted leaves and wood and the wetness of the tree bark. The other two soldiers had already entered into the woods and had begun running in different directions. Just before Jack bowed under the low hanging branches he heard another volley of shots from the five Rebs who were in hot pursuit.

"Just a few more feet to freedom," Jack said out loud. "Just a few more feet to run. Come on, you can do this. Push yourself. Just a few more feet."

Jack never saw the young Reb who fired the shot that tore a large hole in his shoulder and flung his body to the ground with a muffled cry. But he did feel the searing pain in his right shoulder as the lead projectile from the rifle passed through.

As he struck the ground, Jack was keenly aware his world was now changed forever and would never again be the same. He felt the damp grass against his sweaty face, as he lay there motionless for a few moments wondering. Why? He was so close to freedom, he thought. And being able to make it home and see his Jennie.

As the Rebs approached him with their bayonets protruding from their rifles, he no longer had any fear. He looked over at the gaping wound in his right shoulder and managed a forced painful smile for the enemy as they approached and pointed their menacing weapons at his head.

"Looks like I will be sitting out the rest of this here war, Johnny Reb," Jack said, moaning in pain.

"Yep. Looks like one of them-there wounds you can lick as you're a-sitting in Andersonville, Blue Belly," the young Reb snickered.

As Jack looked up at the three Rebs standing around him, the Rebs began to swirl and grow dim and then his world became black.

On June 17, the Federal garrison at Harper's Ferry was abandoned to Maryland Heights across the river, completely clearing the Shenandoah Valley of Union troops. This created an open door for Lee's Army to invade Pennsylvania with- out worrying about his back.

On June 19, 1863, the main units of the Army of Northern Virginia's Second Corps reached Hagerstown, Maryland, 10 miles from the Pennsylvania line. While the Confederates were storming over the parapets at Winchester, still other units were streaming north towards the Potomac River where they would make their crossing into the town of Williamsport, Maryland. Everything was in motion as the dark clouds of the Army of Northern Virginia grew in strength with every mile they covered.

Continuing the swift march, General Ewell sent out one of his divisions under General Early to take the road to Chambersburg and Cashtown. The Rebs felt as if nothing now could stop their advance, with all of the divisions crossing the Pennsylvania line. Nothing but a miracle would stop them, and for the North, a miracle was all that they had left.

Wesley Culp, a long time friend of Jack Skelly, also fought in the battle of Carter's Woods and Winchester but for the Confederacy, as a result of his working in Virginia. Wesley was unaware that over in the Union lines were not only his close friends Jack, William and Billy, but also his brother, William Culp, all from Gettysburg.

William Culp had eluded capture, but the rest of the Gettysburg boys were captured and rounded up in a staging area along the main road into Winchester, along with the wounded Jack Skelly. Early in the morning on the day after the battle of Carter's Woods, Wesley Culp was marching with his victorious division of Ewell's Corps. As the Corps were passing the area where the Union prisoners of war and wounded were being held for a few days before removal to the Deep South, Wesley was astonished and shocked when he happened to see standing along the road his Gettysburg friend Billy Holtzworth.

Wesley ran over to where his friend was standing. "Billy, Billy Holtzworth, it is good to see you!"

"Well, it is not good to see you, Wesley Culp!" Billy snapped back immediately. "You should have stayed with us, Wesley. All of us together, like it was when we were all young friends at school in Gettysburg," Billy said in an anguished voice.

Wesley said nothing as he stood there with his head down in dejection.

"Jack Skelly has been wounded in the shoulder. Doesn't look good for him at all Wesley," Billy advised with tears streaming down his face. "Is there anything you can do to remove him from this wet field and get him into a hospital," he questioned in a concerned voice.

"I believe I can help. Hold on here and I will talk to my sergeant. Maybe we can at least get him away from this God-forsaken area," Wesley answered, as he looked toward his unit.

Billy walked back to where William was washing Jack's wound. "He may lose the arm, Billy," William advised in a sullen voice. "Good thing Jack is still unconscious so as not to feel the pain." William continued to wash the blood off Jack's neck and face along with the dirt and sweat. In a few minutes, Wesley returned with his sergeant, who was carrying a bucket of water and a fresh cloth for a bandage.

After Jack was cleaned and bandaged, four of Wesley's Reb friends carried Jack to the Confederate field hospital close to the bridge where so many Union soldiers had died trying to cross the bridge. As they carried Jack to the field tent, permeating the air everywhere was the sickening, overpowering, awful stench of unburied soldiers and horses. The air was filled with the cries of the many wounded still lying where they fell in battle. Many men would have to wait days before anyone got to them and assisted with some type of medical aid.

After a hasty examination, the stewards had Jack removed to the outside of the tent so he could be transported to the main field hospital in Winchester, where soldiers, both north and south were placed in nice neat rows to await surgery. The soldiers would soon have to show their courage again; only this time it was for the ordeal of crude Civil War surgery.

Wesley and his friends stayed with Jack for a few minutes before they had to go back to their camp one mile outside of Winchester. Jack had regained consciousness and was glad to see his old friend Wesley, and was surprised to find out that he had been moved. Jack was aware that his wound was fatal and that it would only be a matter of time. He had seen enough combat wounds over the last year to understand his fate. However, he was comforted by the thought that in his last hours, all of his close childhood friends would be gathered around him and united.

How strange this is! Jack thought looking at the four Rebs and two Union soldiers standing around his bed.

"Jack, the boys and me have to fetch ourselves back to camp before they send the dogs after us. I will stop back tomorrow morning before we break camp and head north," Wesley whispered in a soft voice as he laid his hand on Jack's hand.

"You take care and get some sleep now. God go with you Jack," William said as they were escorted out of the tent by two guards and taken back to the prisoner holding area.

As he lay there in the hospital bed his mind became filled with many thoughts of Jennie. Somehow he had to get word to her of his fate. She had a right to know. If the Rebs where heading into Pennsylvania, there might be a chance they would get close to Gettysburg.

"When Wesley comes in the morning I will have him assist me in writing a farewell letter to Jennie," Jack said to himself as he looked out of the tent into the night sky. He tried to get some sleep, but it was impossible with the constant pain. Then there were the flies and mosquitoes that continually buzzed around his face. Added to everything else were the cries of the wounded piercing the room and the night.

Lying there, he gazed into the night sky. The stars appeared like large diamonds. In his imagination he chose one of the stars, a beautiful white twinkling star in the western sky. He thought how that star had been twinkling for thousands of years and would continue to do so for another thousand. The star looked like a diamond wedding ring, a ring that represented his eternal love for Jennie. An eternal love, which is too moral nature, what the sun is to the earth. Yes, Jennie would like the ring when she saw it.

His last thoughts before falling asleep were of Jennie wearing that special ring on their wedding day this coming October, as they began their life together.

8
The Letter
June 17, 1863

When Jack awoke the next morning in the Taylor House Field Hospital in Winchester, he slowly became aware that he could no longer feel the sharp pain in his shoulder wound. Either he had been given something during the night or his wound was beyond pain. Jack believed the latter was what really had taken place.

He also noticed he had been moved from the field tent outside the building to a bed inside the Taylor House Hospital, and his blood-soaked clothes had been removed. The human cries of pain reminded him to be thankful that he did not have to endure the excruciating pain of amputation.

Jack felt very fortunate as he observed the man in the bed across from his who had lost both legs. At least he would be able to die in one piece. Amputation was always in the mind of the soldier no matter what his rank or position, he thought. No soldier wanted to end up losing a limb because gangrene had set in.

For Jack, his only concern was to write his farewell letter to Jennie and pray this letter would find its way to Gettysburg. As he lay there in bed, the letter motivated his every thought. Jack did not want to leave this world without saying good-bye to the one person who meant the most to him.

When his friend Wesley found Jack on the battlefield, Jack took this as a sign that God was giving him a chance to say good-bye, and make his peace. What are the chances, Jack thought, of Wesley finding him among thousands of men scattered about the field of battle.

The morning passed slowly and Jack was becoming increasingly worried that he had missed Wesley. He was also very thirsty. The wooden canteen of water Wesley left last evening was empty, and Jack prayed that his friend would come soon.

As Jack waited, he closed his eyes and went over in his mind the words he was going to share with Jennie. He tried to picture Jennie reading the letter and her reaction to the sad news. He could clearly see her standing there in her bedroom sitting on the bed reading his letter. Jack fell asleep with those thoughts and was awakened by Wesley's soft-spoken "Hello, Jack," and gentle nudge.

Jack opened his eyes and tried to smile. Wesley was standing at his side along with three of his friends from their Stonewall unit. He held up Jack's head and gave him some water from another canteen. Then Wesley placed the canteen on the stand next to the bed so Jack would have water when needed.

"How do you feel today, Jack? Your color seems to be good," Wesley announced as he checked Jack's wound for maggots and flies.

"We will be leaving in about an hour. Is there anything you would like for me to do before we pull out?" Wesley questioned.

"Yes, there is one thing, Wesley," Jack whispered in a horse voice. "I would like to dictate a letter to be given to Jennie Wade if you make it to Gettysburg. This letter must be given to Jennie and Jennie only," Jack declared firmly.

"You know I will honor your wishes, Jack," Wesley avowed. "You have my word it will be given to Jennie and no one else," Wesley affirmed in a steady voice.

"Good," Jack said as he nodded his head. "Now, if you will check my bag you will find some paper and a small pencil." As Wesley was looking for paper and pencil, one of the Rebs standing in front of the bed spoke up.

"Next time you Blue Bellies fight, it had better be with a little more spunk than youins did yesterday. We heard tell Old Man Milroy is still running," he joked. Jack smiled and nodded his head; the war was over for him so the Reb's comment did not brother him at all.

Wesley removed the paper and pencil from his bag and pulled up a chair alongside the bed as his friends stood behind him. "I guess we are ready if you are, Jack," Wesley stated in a hurried voice.

"Well, I don't want to be a holding up the Army of Northern Virginia now, do I?" Jack questioned with his broad smile.

Jack turned his head toward Wesley and said, "I believe I am ready." Wesley removed his broad-brimmed hat and then the solders standing behind Wesley removed their hats.

"My dearest Jennie;" Jack paused as if choked up.

"It is with some difficulty I am writing this letter to you, however, the Almighty has given me the strength and clear mind to share my feelings with you in my last hours on earth. A few days ago I was mortally wounded outside of Winchester Virginia at a place called Carter's Woods. Our childhood friends William Ziegler and Billy Holtzworth and I were captured together and held prisoners. Please try and forgive me for this foolish act, but I tried to escape along

with two other soldiers. Jennie, I almost made the escape. After I was wounded my friends carried me to a tree along the main road into Winchester. As Billy was standing along the road talking to William Ziegler, another friend of ours, Wesley Culp, who is fighting for the Rebs, saw Billy and ran over to say hello. I know it is difficult to believe we would all meet like this after fighting each other all day. No one ever said war was sensible and right.

Wesley and some of his Reb friends carried me to a field tent in Winchester where I could be taken care of. If our friend Wesley did not come along when he did, I would have died right there under that tree. Yes, God has seen fit to lengthen my life a few more days in order to write you my Farewell letter." Jack paused, and looking up at the ceiling gave Wesley time to catch up.

"I know now Jennie, everything that you read to me by the twin springs this past April was true and the times we shared together since childhood will never be lost. The memory of all the blissful moments we have had together come hovering over me each night. And now it is

very difficult for me to give them up; as ashes in the wind.

You and I will always be part of each other, no matter what happens. The words we spoke, the pledges we gave to each other, the intimate moments will never die; as our love will never die. You see Jennie; I know now our love can't die. Our love will always be present.

If I could change any of the past I would have married you before I left in April. Then maybe you would be carrying our child as a living part of our love; but that was not meant to be.

You made the difference in my life by giving me purpose, hope and love. I love you now as I will love you forever, and nothing can take that love away from us. Nothing, not even death." Jack again paused, allowing Wesley time to catch up. He observed other soldiers, both Blue and Gray, gathered around the bed listening to this very unusual event. Jack continued.

"Thank you Jennie, for your faith and support and your undying love. It was wonderful to know that someone out there cared. Forgive me of my many faults

and shortcomings and the pains I have caused you. I am truly sorry.

Jennie, if the dead can come back to this earth and gather around those they love, I shall always be near you in darkness and in light. Remember my love. 'Though nothing can bring back the hour of splendor in the grass, of glory in the flower; we will grieve not, rather find strength in what remains behind.'

Yes Jennie, there was a time. And, it was our time and we loved to the fullest, and our time together has been a wonderful dance. Thank you. God go with you, my love, until we meet again.

Always, Jack

With the letter completed, Jack now felt at peace, peace with God and his fellow man. He rolled over on his back and sighed. There was not a dry eye in the room.

Wesley wiped away tears that ran down his dirt-caked face, folded the letter and placed the precious item in a wax-wrapped envelope. He then placed the envelope in the inner pocket of his gray uniform patting it with a tender touch.

"No one but Jennie will receive this letter," he vowed. "God go with you, my friend," Wesley whispered to Jack as he embraced him.

"Good-bye and God go with you too, Wesley. When this here war is over we will all get together some time down the road. It will be like old times."

They parted knowing that that would be the last time they would ever see one another again. However, they both knew life was full of separations; from the moment of birth to the moment of death.

The Rebs all said their good-byes to Jack, and then turned and began walking out of the hot, humid room. Jack watched until they were all out of sight.

"Good-bye old friend," Jack whispered. He looked around the room for a few moments and then lay back down. In the other rooms he could hear the wounded calling out for water and help. At least he would not die alone because he had plenty of company all around him. His memories went back to Jennie and to Gettysburg and the moments they had shared together the last week before he left.

Jack's mind became far removed from the war, the killing, the pain and the sorrow of separation. The war no longer mattered to Jack. Who would win, or who would lose was no longer of any consequence to him. He could not see the gathering storm of soldiers passing by his window, heading down the long dusty road to their destinies.

For Jack Skelly, the passing troops meant nothing. He was not even watching as the line of soldiers went by, marching to the beat of muffled drums. He was far away. He was back at Spangler's spring and McAllister's Woods with Jennie. He was lying in the cool, tall spear grass alongside her warm, tender body, looking up at the walnut trees as they spread their wonderful limbs across the sky.

A gentle April breeze blew softly across their bodies, and all around them the fragrance of spring flowers permeated the fresh air. It was early spring. The world was filled with life; the promise of a new birth was everywhere; the promise of things to come and a warm full summer of abundance and life.

Life, he thought for a moment.

Yes, that is what life is, Jack thought. Life has been a wonderful dance.

Thank you God.

9
The Muffled Drums
June 26-30, 1863

On June 20, 1863, Pennsylvania was suddenly seized with statewide panic as news of General Lee's approaching army reached the streets of its towns. Pennsylvania Governor Andrew Curtain added to the panic by distributing handbills declaring, "The Enemy is approaching." The Governor was trying to persuade other state militia to come to the defense of Pennsylvania. The good Governor also sent telegraphed warnings directing people to move their stores as soon as possible.

The appeal for help from the Governor mustered some 50,000 men. The numbers were impressive, but their effectiveness in attempting to stop Lee's army was equivalent to a small bee sting slowing down a bull.

Adding to the stress and panic for the citizens of Gettysburg, General Couch sent a telegram on June 20, 1863, alerting the residents in towns along the Pennsylvania line to prepare for their own defense. Gettysburg's newspapers also added to the confusion as to what was happening with Lee's invasion by publishing contradictory statements. Jennie noticed the citizens of Gettysburg did little during the day other than stand in the streets and discuss the latest news and events taking shape.

On June 24th, 1863, the Confederates marched into Chambersburg, with the regimental band playing "Bonnie Blue Flag." The muffled drums could be heard throughout the day as the long lines of wagon trains, herds of cattle and columns of infantry passed through the town. The citizens, mostly curious women wanting to see what southern Rebs looked like, stood along the streets and sat in the windows to get a closer look. The women also enjoyed taunting the soldiers with catcalls, jeers and flag-waving as the Reb army passed by.

In Gettysburg, the news of the advancing Rebs reached the citizens within hours after the army marched through. Chambersburg and the news of the advancing Rebs sent Gettysburg into a frenzy of terror.

The majority of the colored citizens of Adams County gathered whatever possessions they could carry and departed quickly on their horses in the opposite direction of the advancing Rebs. A few merchants like the Fahnestock Brothers and Mr. Schick, moved their merchandise to waiting boxcars bound for Philadelphia. Banks removed their valuables and all courthouse records were packed away in boxes and hidden in safe places.

Yet in spite of the many rumors, the majority of the citizens continued to work in their backyard gardens and tend to their flowerbeds as if nothing were happening. Many believed the Rebs were never coming to the Gettysburg area, and lost faith in any of the news filtering through to the town.

Even Georgia stayed in her backyard garden in the early mornings tending to her flowers and vegetables. She loved to work in her garden, especially with the flowers that surrounded the edge of the garden, giving it color when in full bloom. One of the many rumors spreading through Gettysburg was that the Confederates ate children when they could not find food. Jennie found that to be disgusting and could not believe any human would ever commit such an act. However, to be on the safe side, Jennie would make sure she watched her young brothers very closely if the Rebs came to town.

In spite of the pandemonium over the last several days, Jennie experienced an electrifying chill of excitement over the possibility of seeing Jack. He could be on his way with the army right now, Jennie thought. However, she did not want to get her hopes up that Jack's unit would be sent here if the Rebs did show up in the Gettysburg area.

On the evening of June 23th, sitting on the bench just outside the kitchen door while visiting Georgia, Jennie noticed many of the blacks of Gettysburg leaving town.

"The blacks I heard are leaving Gettysburg every day by the dozens. Must be mighty scared of something," Jennie theorized out loud to Georgia.

"The blacks don't have much to concern themselves with. Lee's army ain't going to make it this far-east," Georgia assured Jennie.

"You are probably right, George. But the stories and rumors I have been hearing on the streets scare the devil right out of me."

"In some ways, I am praying that the Rebs do come to our town because…"

"Jennie! Jennie Wade! What are you saying? Don't let anyone hear you say that," Georgia interrupted as she looked around to see if anyone overheard her sister. "Those are not words to be spreading around the town at this time. Do you hear me?"

"Yes, George, I understand what you are saying. If you would let me finish, I was about to say that if the Rebs come to Gettysburg, then I am quite sure Jack and the 87th Pennsylvania will be in the mix," Jennie exclaimed in a loud voice.

"George, that means Jack, could be here in Gettysburg! Think of that. Jack Skelly defending our little town."

"Now, don't you go and get your hopes up with that thought, Jennie. Chances are, you will not see Jack until this fall."

Jennie did not answer her sister. She leaned back against the brick building and closed her eyes. In her imagination Jack was coming to Gettysburg and Jennie would be waiting for him when the 87th marched proudly into town.

On Friday, June 26, 1863, as General Ewell's Rebs were gathering what requisitions they could in Chambersburg, General Early's division had a little scrap with a small group of state militia west of Gettysburg. After a brief exchange of shots, the militia vanished into the surrounding countryside and the Rebs continued their march into Gettysburg along Chambersburg Street, with 175 prisoners they had gathered up along the way.

The sight of Rebs on their street, firing their guns in every direction and pushing prisoners along with their bayonets and horrid yells, sent the citizens of Gettysburg into complete shock and disbelief. Many hid in their cellars until the invading apocalyptic hordes from hell left their town. A few of the women could not handle the sight of the Rebs walking freely through their town and fainted on the sidewalks.

The Rebs were covered with dust and their faces smeared with dirt and grime. Many were barefoot and their uniforms of butternut and light gray were tattered, with patches over the worn areas.

No one could believe the towns greatest fears had become a reality. The Rebs began spreading rumors throughout the town about a great victory at Winchester.

Jennie had been standing in the town square with a group of women when she heard the news of what happened in Winchester, Virginia.

"How many Blue Bellies in this here town?" barked one bearded private covered with dust to a small group of women gathered on the square. When all of the women, who were too scared to say anything at all, stood speechless, the young private roared out. "All you women there, now move along or we will take you prisoner." He smiled and Jennie could see his missing teeth and blackened gums.

"Iff'n you believe your Blue Belly soldiers will come and help you, well don't you go counting on that at all. The same licking will be given to this town as we done to Winchester," the young Reb bellowed out to the women, who were near panic with fear of being molested.

"What happened at Winchester," Jennie shouted out before the Reb turned to leave.

"Your troops scattered like fallen leaves before us. Killed many Blue Bellies, took many more as prisoners. The same will happen again if your Blue Bellies show up here," he shouted back to the women. "Now get back to your homes, go ahead now, and skedaddle."

Jennie was stunned. Jack was stationed outside of Winchester. Then again, maybe he had been transferred to another company or location.

"Jack's brother Dan might know something. I will walk over to their store and find out what happened. Can't believe a word the Rebs say anyhow," Jennie bantered to herself out loud.

On the way to the Skelly store Jennie ran into Dan, who was heading up to the Town Square to see what the Rebs were up to.

"Dan, have you heard anything from Jack? There has been a battle fought in Winchester and..."

"Slow down, Jennie," Dan interrupted. "There's been talk all over town this afternoon about a battle fought last week sometime and...well...our boys turned and ran off the field of battle. I guess there was so much confusion during the fight that hundreds of our boys were captured."

"Dan, what are you saying?" Jennie fired right back.

"I am telling you the 87th Pennsylvania up and got a terrible whipping at Winchester, that is all I know at this time."

"I can't believe the 87th would run..."

"Believe it, Jennie," Dan interrupted as he began running toward the square.

"Believe it!"

Events were happening too fast for Jennie. She would have to take some time in understanding what Dan had shared with her. For now, Jennie could not believe the 87th would run.

The Rebs pitched camp outside of the town early in the evening. They wanted to get a good start in the morning to their major objective: the town of York. The Rebs felt that York would yield the Confederacy greater booty than Gettysburg.

Immediately after the news of the advancing Confederates reached Adams County and Gettysburg, an emergency regiment consisting of students from the Lutheran Seminary and Pennsylvania College was formed.

Because John Wade was not a student he could not join up with these units; however, he did manage to volunteer in the 21st Pennsylvania Cavalry Regiment on June 23rd. After weeks of haranguing his mother to allow him to join, he finally persuaded his mother to permit him to join the Cavalry.

Jennie remained totally against her mother's decision, stating John was far too young to fight Rebs. However, John went ahead with his plans to become the bugler for his company in spite of Jennie's protest.

Because of his small stature of five feet three inches, when John's uniform arrived on June 24th, it was two sizes too large. John begged Jennie to make the necessary alterations on his uniform before his company left Gettysburg for scouting duty.

Two hours before the Confederates rode into Gettysburg, John's company left to join up with another unit to scout the area along the Pennsylvania line. The unit left in such a hurry they could not wait for John's uniform to be completed and he was left behind. After John badgered his sister to hurry, Jennie finally completed his uniform just as the dust was settling from the quick departure of his panic-stricken cavalry unit.

"Thanks, Jennie, for helping me with my uniform," John said as he turned to leave. "I won't forget your help," he avowed. He mounted his horse, waved good-bye to Jennie and his mother and hurriedly began riding to catch up with his company in his newly altered uniform.

Jennie turned to her mother and in a calm voice stated, "I don't believe I shall ever see John again."

"Yes you will, Jennie. We will all see our John James again. You shouldn't say things like that. Its bad luck you know," her mother retorted. "I believe we have some more uniforms to alter today, and by the looks of things around town we had better hurry," her mother exclaimed. Jennie stood there for a few moments watching John disappear down the road.

In the town square around the same moment John Wade rode down Emmitsburg Road, the town constable, John Lawrence Burns, was taking a message from General Early to the acting Burgess, David Kendlehardt, in relation to Confederate demands and requisitions. Since the demands could not be met because town provisions were low and most of the goods and money had been shipped to other locations, the Rebs began collecting all serviceable horses in the village.

James Pierce asked Samuel Wade, who was employed as a delivery boy by the Pierce family, if he would ride their favorite family horse out of town to save it from the thieving Rebs. Samuel, who was a member of the "Gettysburg Zouaves," a semi-military club, was more than willing to help the Pierces. For a 12-year-old boy, this assignment was the closest he would come to fighting the Rebs, and he could not resist the challenge.

Samuel ran home to let his mother and Jennie know about the mission he would be on. Both insisted Samuel stay at home.

"Listen to us, Sam," Jennie pleaded. "The Rebs are all about the town and they are arresting any one who is trying to hide horses or possessions. This is too dangerous!"

"I don't believe they will waste time on a 12- year-old boy and his horse. The Rebs have better things to go after than me," Samuel argued. "Now I'd better leave. I will be careful Mother, I promise. I shall only be gone for about an hour," he exclaimed as he walked out the door.

"Samuel! You come back here right now! It's not safe on the streets!" Jennie yelled as her brother ran down the street and back to Mr. Pierce's shop. Samuel told Mr. Pierce it was all right with his mother and sister to ride the horse out of town to safety.

"I am going to hold the Pierces responsible if anything happens to that boy," Jennie advised her mother.

At 7:30 in the morning, as Samuel was riding out of Gettysburg on Baltimore Street on the iron-gray horse, his older sister, Georgia, went into her first stages of labor pains. Mrs. Catharine McClain, the occupant in the other half of the double house where Georgia lived, ran down to get Mrs. Wade. The town doctor had already been sent for, and Mrs. McClain felt that Georgia needed help until the doctor arrived. Mary Wade left immediately, placing Jennie in charge of the responsibilities of taking care of the boys and their home on Breckenridge Street.

Around 9:00 in the morning, Jennie began to worry about Samuel, and she also wanted to find out how Georgia was doing. She left the house and began walking down Breckenridge Street to the corner of Baltimore Street where the Pierces lived, holding hands with young Isaac on one side and Harry on the other.

"Where is that boy?" she questioned to herself out loud. "Wait till I fetch that boy home. He is going to get the thrashing of his life."

Jennie stood on the corner of Breckenridge Street and Baltimore Street looking for Samuel. With each passing minute Jennie was becoming more fearful something terrible had happened to her brother. The longer she stood there, the more she blamed the Pierces for allowing Samuel to go on such a dangerous mission today.

"Heaven's sake Miss. Wade, what are you doing standing here on the corner of the street with Rebs running about shooting their guns off?" Anna Garlach inquired.

"I am looking for my brother Samuel. He left more than an hour ago on a horse he was going to hide from the Rebs," Jennie stated in a concerned voice.

Baltimore Street was filled with billows of gray dust, stirred up by the passing Rebs pulling what livestock they could to the Town Square. The dust was settling on their clothes as the two women stood there talking.

"There is no way I am about to let a bunch of low-down Reb thieves enter my house, take all my possessions and then pay me in paper money that is worthless," Anna thundered out to a passing Reb carrying a basket full of fresh eggs.

"Them Rebs will burn in hell, Jennie, for this destruction they have done to our town. May you burn in hell for ever, Johnny Reb, you..."

"Anna! You had better watch what you are saying in front of these Rebs," Jennie stated. Before she could continue, Jennie saw Samuel being led down Baltimore Street by two Rebs on the very horse he had tried to save. The soldiers were making their way to the town square where all the goods and animals were being gathered.

Jennie knew immediately Samuel was a prisoner of war. Jennie exploded in anger with the vision of her brother being led down the street by the enemy.

Before Jennie could move, Mrs. Pierce beckoned to one of the Rebs leading the horse Samuel was riding.

"You don't want the boy! He is only living with us as a helper in our store," Mrs. Pierce proclaimed to the Rebs in a strong voice. She had been watching the street from her front parlor window when she saw Samuel and their horse being led down the street and past their home.

Jennie ran up to the Reb holding the horse and began pounding on his arm, yelling, "You damn Rebs! Can't you see he is only a small boy; why don't you pick on someone your own size?" Jennie yelled. "You're lower than a snake's belly."

The soldier looked at her and smiled, showing his toothless, dirty grin. He brushed her aside and continued down the street laughing. The other soldier walking behind the horse answered Mrs. Pierce's question by stating, "We have no need of the boy; he will be released up at the town square unharmed."

Tensions rose as Jennie now confronted Mrs. Pierce. "You are responsible for this, you and your family. If the Rebs take our Sam, I don't know what I'll do with you folks!" Jennie avowed in a strong voice. Mrs. Pierce turned and walked back to her house, and Jennie made her way to Georgia's house to get help from her mother with Samuel's release.

As Jennie walked down to her sister's house, she had a difficult time carrying Isaac and trying to hold on to Harry, who was enthralled with the entire excitement taking place around him.

Breathing fast and hard Jennie could hardly speak as she entered the kitchen, and to her surprise found that Georgia had delivered a healthy baby boy just before her arrival. The doctor and Mary Wade had a difficult time trying to save the baby. The cord had been wrapped around the baby's neck in the birth canal. In spite of this near tragedy, a healthy baby was welcomed into the world. Georgia's bed had been brought down earlier that spring from the upstairs bedroom, allowing her to be on the first floor without going up and down the stairs.

Jennie did not want to scare an already weakened Georgia and asked her mother to step outside for some important news about Samuel.

"Can't this wait until another time Jennie?" her mother questioned.

"I think you need to know what has happened to Samuel," Jennie whispered softly in her mother's ear.

Outside the house, Jennie related the complete story of what happened on Baltimore Street. "I really feel you should go up to the town square and get the release of Samuel. They will listen to a mother better than a sister. You need to go now!" Jennie exhorted.

Mary Wade left immediately, leaving Jennie to care for Georgia and the baby. Jennie gave the excuse their mother was needed back home.

"Something had come up George," Jennie claimed, "that needed their mother's attention." Georgia was too exhausted to question her sister for details, and fell asleep with the baby cradled in her arms.

At the Town Square Mrs. Wade appeared before General Early, who set up a temporary camp on the square. Mary Wade explained the situation to the General, who was very compassionate and concerned about the boy, and had Samuel released immediately with the South's apology. However, the horse now belonged to the Army of Northern Virginia.

A few minutes after Mrs. Wade left with Samuel, Mr. Pierce appeared before Colonel White and pleaded for the return of the beloved family horse. The request was denied. Colonel White had been informed the Pierce family was "staunch Black Abolitionists" with sons in the Union Army. The Pierce family felt that it was Jennie Wade and her mother that was the source of Colonel White's information. The Pierce family would never forgive Jennie and began to spread rumors that the Wades were southern sympathizers.

As they approached Breckenridge Street, Mary Wade could hear the clock on the courthouse striking four p.m. It was late Friday afternoon, June 26, 1863. This would be a day and time Mary Wade would never forget as she placed her arm around Samuel and gave him a huge hug.

"Did you see any signs that the Rebs were staying in Gettysburg," Jennie questioned her mother as they walked into the kitchen.

"No, I believe the Rebs will be leaving as soon as everything they can steal has been removed from the stores and homes," Mary Wade answered.

Jennie's heart sank with the thought of the Rebs leaving. If they go, she thought, our soldiers will have no reason to come here and I won't get to see Jack. As the family walked back to Georgia's house, the last of the Rebs passed by on the way out of town. By eight the next morning, Saturday, June 27th, the Confederates had left and were heading toward York, hopefully for richer plunder for the army. The consensus of the citizens of Gettysburg was declared by the main newspaper, The Compiler: "Their deportment generally was civil." Everyone in Gettysburg heaved a collective sigh of relief; everyone that is except Jennie Wade.

On Monday, June 29, 1863, the Compiler reported that a Confederate army of approximately 13,000 men had made camp five miles northeast of Gettysburg. That evening the citizens of Gettysburg could see the Reb campfires scattered along the slopes of South Mountain. The campfires were not a good sight to behold. Once again tension and fear gripped the streets as the town citizens poured out into the streets to discuss the events of the day.

The last day of June, Tuesday, June 30, 1863, was again filled with surprises for the citizens of Gettysburg. On every corner there were small gatherings of people sharing and exchanging stories. Many of the citizens decided to move their possessions to their basements just in case the Rebs would return with a vengeance. However, most of Gettysburg acted as if the Rebs were not coming back into town, and celebrations sprang up everywhere with groups of girls singing patriotic songs. People had mixed feelings as to what the Rebs were up to just five miles outside of their town.

With the Rebs gone from the town Jennie had become withdrawn. The hope of seeing Jack had vanished and the rumors of what really happened at Winchester began to haunt her.

Mary Wade decided to stay a week with Georgia and the baby. Jennie would take care of their home on Breckenridge Street while watching her brothers Samuel and Harry, and their boarder Isaac Brinkerhoff.

Jennie's spirits were lifted when the news reached her that the vanguard of Union General John Buford's 1st Cavalry Division, sent ahead by General John Reynolds, had arrived in Gettysburg around 11:00.

The gloom and fear that had prevailed over the town over the last several days had now changed to one of rejoicing by the citizens. The decision to send Buford's Cavalry Division was made by General Reynolds when he learned that the Southern Divisions of General A.P. Hill and General Longstreet were heading toward Chambersburg.

General Buford arrived just in time to make contact with a few scouts from General Pettigew's brigade in Heath's Division. General Heath had sent Pettigew's men to Gettysburg to find shoes for the army. Instead of coming into Gettysburg the Rebs sighted Buford's Cavalry on the outskirts of the town and withdrew to Cashtown.

Jennie was delighted with the news that the Union Army had finally arrived. In anticipation of the enemy's return, Buford set up a defense perimeter west of Gettysburg. He was convinced that on the morning of July 1st, the Rebs would attack.

As the head of the cavalry column approached the intersection of South Washington Street, the tired and dusty soldiers were surprised by the reception of patriotic songs and flag-waving by young beautiful girls in long calico dresses. The citizens were excited to have the Army in their town. They felt safe and secure for the first time in weeks. Many of the families invited the soldiers into their homes for a home-cooked meal.

Anna Garlach and Florie Culp tried to get Jennie to join them as they stood alongside the street singing. Jennie declined the invitation due to the care of Isaac who was having trouble adjusting to all the excitement over the past several days.

"You sing for me, Anna," Jennie exhorted as she rocked Isaac to sleep. "My heart and soul are with our boys in blue, but I just can't leave home afearin' Isaac might have a seizure."

The girls left Jennie rocking Isaac and made their way to Washington Street where the women of Gettysburg were singing to the troops as they rode by. General Buford enjoyed the celebration, but in the back of his mind he knew all Hell would break out in the morning. For now he would allow his troops some peace and joy, knowing that come morning many of them would soon be dead.

The moon rose bright and clear over Gettysburg on the last night in June. Jennie had tucked the boys into bed early and sat on the front porch looking into the expanses of the night sky. She looked intently at the moon, thinking Jack could possibly be looking at the moon at the same time. The moon was their physical connection; their bond. The moon had been visible on their last night together as they exchanged their goodbyes.

"Jack, if you are looking at this moon tonight, remember, I love you. I will always love you," Jennie whispered.

Let's see, Jennie thought, tomorrow is the first day of July. Yes, maybe tomorrow God will bring Jack back to me. Yes, the first day...Jennie went into a sound asleep.

The summer night air was fresh as the crickets broke the stillness with their chorus of night sounds; sounds that brought a deep sleep and good dreams to the citizens of Gettysburg.

10
The First Day
July 1, 1863

The early morning of the first day in July arrived with a sky speckled intermittently with clouds on a background of translucent pink and rose colors. A gentle breeze barely moved the leaves on the trees. The temperature hovered around 70 degrees this early in the morning.

By seven o'clock, Jennie had been up for an hour. She sensed something was different. As Jennie stood by the open kitchen door she noticed an uncommon silence. The silence permeated the air and pierced her soul with a hidden fear. Jennie noticed not one bird was singing or any dogs barking. It appeared the birds and animals were aware of something that was about to take place, something terrible and horrible.

Jennie shuddered, with small goose bumps appearing over her arms. As she turned to go into the house, she thought she heard the distant booming sound of thunder.

"Could that be thunder?" she questioned out loud to herself. "I did not think it was to rain today." She walked out on the front porch and noticed many of her neighbors were gathering on the street looking in the direction of north. Over on the northern horizon a loud, booming, ominous sound sent terror in the hearts of all who stood there in the street. They knew the sound was not thunder; what they were hearing was the booming sound of cannons.

A few minutes later, Jennie heard the sounds of what she thought could be that of a muzzle-loading rifle with their staccato beat, pop...pop...pop...pop. The sound was then answered by a continued loud bang... bang...bang...bang...bang of Yankee carbines. And in the background one could hear the booming of more cannons.

Women on the streets began to cry; others screamed in fear. As her neighbors ran back into their homes, Jennie stood in the street; her soul filled with excitement and yet fear. In a few moments a shell burst overhead, sending little bits of metal over the street and in her hair.

Jennie ran into her house and slammed the door shut. She ran upstairs to the boy's bedroom only to find them hanging out the window looking north. Billows of black and gray smoke began to rise about the tree line northwest of town.

Another boom from a cannon; this one was closer, and they could feel the vibrations tingle through their bodies. Then there was a succession of booms, one after another as if the world was breaking apart. The boys all headed under the bed for protection. Isaac hugged Jennie tight and would not let go.

"You boys get dressed right now," Jennie shouted. "I am going to dress Isaac. Now get out from underneath the bed and get dressed or you both are going to get the switch," she threatened. Her voice was tense but she hoped the boys could not detect she was afraid.

In moments the boys were clothed and gathered in the kitchen. After dressing little Isaac, Jennie went down to the kitchen and prepared breakfast. Every once in a while Jennie could see people carrying personal belongings while hurrying down the street. Standing on the porch, she saw some of her neighbors descending into their root cellars.

On the north side of Gettysburg the noise of battle had increased, with the deafening sounds of cannons booming. The noise was enough to send the fear of God into any atheist still alive on the field.

Jennie gathered the boys under the kitchen table. Together they began to pray for God's mercy and protection. "Dear God please preserve us in this hour of danger, watch over your children and shelter us under your wing..."

Her prayer was interrupted when a shell exploded above the house next to their house, sending lead fragments on the roofs of the homes. Isaac screamed. Even Samuel huddled close to Jennie as tears came streaming down his face.

After an hour of kneeling under the kitchen table Jennie noticed shelling from the Confederate batteries west of town began to explode more often inside the town. Neighbors who had root cellars had gathered in them when the battle began, others fled to their basements for protection. Ben Harden, a close neighbor to the Wades, invited Jennie and the boys into his root cellar until the fighting was over.

Jennie had decided long before Ben came to her door, she would take the boys to Georgia's house south of Gettysburg to get away from the fighting in the north. At Georgia's house far away from the fighting there would be no immediate danger, and probably one could not even hear the sound of the cannons, Jennie thought.

"Thanks Ben for the offer of safety, but I am going to take the boys to my sister's house at the south end of town where we will be completely safe until this is over," Jennie proclaimed.

"Your family has been good to my wife and me. Nothing will ever be the same again for us," he said looking north in the direction of the noise of battle. "God go with you Jennie Wade."

"God go with you too Ben," Jennie answered as he turned and walked back to his house.

The clock on the kitchen wall announced it was 11:00. Jennie had no time to spare if she wanted to get the boys to safety in her sister's house. Jennie knew the trip down to Georgia's house would be difficult with three boys, and a change of clothes.

"Listen to me very carefully. Each of you is to stay close to me and not wander away. Do you all understand?" Jennie questioned with a stressed voice.

"Yes. We understand," the boys said all together.

"Jennie, I would like to stay with the Pierces. They have a deep cellar, large enough for all of us to stay in," Samuel explained. Just the mention of the name Pierce sent a flash of anger through Jennie, but she did not want the boys to notice.

"Yes, if you want to stay with them you can. But I am going to take Harry and Isaac to Georgia's." There was no way she wanted to spend two or three days cooped up with the Pierces.

Leaving her house, she locked the door behind her chuckling to herself at the thought of locking the Rebs out of her house. As she dropped the house key into her dress pocket, Jennie felt the key resting against the picture of Jack she carried with her wherever she went. Jennie removed the picture from her pocket and looked at Jack for a few moments. This practice gave her a sense of his continued presence no matter where she would find herself. Tears welled up in her eyes, and for a few moments blurred her vision.

"Come on boys. Let's be on our way. This whole mess will be straightened out very soon. This will all pass," she exhorted.

"Come on Jennie let's get out of here!" Harry screamed as a shell burst overhead. Everywhere there were loud booming noises as if someone had opened the door to Hell and all the demons were loose onto the streets of Gettysburg.

As Jennie and the boys turned onto Baltimore Street they were almost run over by a military wagon filled with soldiers cursing at them to get off the streets and into a cellar. The streets were crowded from pavement to pavement with hundreds of dust-covered soldiers of every description from the Union 11th, Corps.

Mingled in with the soldiers were the wagons pulled by horses, which jumped in fear every time there was a distant boom. As the soldiers passed, Jennie and the boys could see in the faces of the soldiers, fear and terror. The mass of humanity was all moving in one direction; toward the north end of town. Jennie was glad they were walking in the opposite direction away from the noise of battle, the pain, and the death she knew awaited the soldiers.

As they approached the red brick house of their sister, Harry ran ahead and disappeared through the door. A few moments later when Jennie entered, she found the family all gathered around Georgia's bed as she fed the baby. Jennie spent a few minutes sharing the experiences of the morning and then began working in the kitchen.

"How much bread do you think we need, Mother, over the next several days?" Jennie questioned.

"I would mix up enough dough for at least 10 loaves of bread. And have Harry fetch enough wood in for at least four good fires," Mary Wade suggested as she folded bedclothes.

No one knew how long they would be holed up in the house and Mary wanted to make sure her family would not be exposed to the outside. She felt the family was safe as long as they were in the thick brick building.

Jennie started the yeast, mixing it into a flour sponge, allowing the yeast to rise. After the flour sponge had risen it would bake in the oven for around one hour. Jennie made enough dough for 10 loaves, but she knew they would only last a few days with all of the mouths to feed in the house.

By one o'clock in the afternoon, the temperature had climbed into the mid-seventies. The afternoon was cloudy with no breeze and very hot and humid. Many of the soldiers who had just arrived in Gettysburg were in need of water, and many of the citizens were out along the streets with pails of cool water for the thirsty soldiers.

After Jennie noticed the yeast was rising, she decided to help the soldiers she witnessed from the kitchen window. She walked out to the windless well along the east side of the house and began filling buckets with refreshing water for the cavalrymen resting in a small open field near the east side of the house. Both horses and men drank all they could, as Jennie made trip after trip to the deep well. Her green dress became drenched from the waist down, and beads of perspiration began dripping from her face and hair.

As the early afternoon progressed, word spread through the soldiers in the surrounding area that a beautiful young girl was providing water.

"One bucket is not going to do the job," Jennie muttered to herself as she descended into the basement to bring up another bucket. "Harry!" Jennie shouted above the distant sounds of battle. "I need your help in giving out the water. There are just too many men out here." The little red brick house had become a stop for refreshment in water and bread for hundreds of Union soldiers retreating to Cemetery Hill.

Harry, who had been in the basement stairway watching the hundreds of soldiers passing by the house, came up and began pumping water into the buckets using the long pump handle. When one bucket was full Jennie would come over and replace it with the empty one. The bucket brigade was working out just fine for both brother and sister, and Harry enjoyed playing in the water, watching the entire war action taking place around him.

Around three o'clock, with the temperature climbing into the high seventies, the main Union lines gave way to superior

Confederate forces north and northwest of Gettysburg. The entire 11th Corps began a quick retreat, which uncovered the right flank and rear of the 1st Corps. Together both Corps began a retreat through the streets of Gettysburg, as yelling Confederates followed in hot pursuit.

Union officers rode through the town ordering all civilians into their basements or cellars. The wild scramble through Gettysburg was in full swing. The soldiers who survived the run through the streets regrouped with other remnants of different units on top of Cemetery Hill just south of the town. Cemetery Hill was the only hope in stopping a total disaster for the entire Union Army.

The streets were clogged as horses, wagons and soldiers were caught up in colliding regiments in total chaos. Shells began exploding in the town as bricks from the homes and the streets began flying in every direction. Soldiers from both Corps converged in Gettysburg at the same time, which increased the pandemonium.

The panic-stricken citizens begged the Union soldiers running past them not to abandon the town to the hordes of wicked Rebs. A few of the citizens tried to stop the soldiers from running away by holding on to their arms or legs. To the citizens of Gettysburg, the retreat through their town was an absolute nightmare.

Jennie learned later that evening, from a soldier she had given some bread to, that "The majority of our boys found themselves hopelessly lost in them dead-end alleys and blocked streets, Miss." The old soldier anguished, "Truth be known, Miss, when them Rebs followed right after our boys through the town streets things got real vicious- like."

The soldier removed his dusty cap and scratched his matted hair as he continued, "Them there Rebs, well, they must of took hundreds of our boys prisoners. The boys you see, plain and simple, just did not have anywhere to go in them streets." Jennie stood there shaking her head in disbelief and fought back her tears.

"I even heard tell some of our boys being shot in the back even when they were trying to surrender. Never saw anything like it, Miss! The Rebs were like demons gone mad." The soldier replaced his cap and stood up. "Thank you, Miss, for the bread and water, I shall never forget your kindness," the soldier remarked as he turned and walked toward Cemetery Hill where thousands of his brothers in arms were gathering.

Inside the safety of the brick house, Mary Wade was busy preparing food for her family gathered within. The 10 loaves of bread that

Jennie had prepared earlier had been divided up and given to the soldiers by Jennie. Mrs. Wade had begun to mix the yeast in preparation for another 10 loaves of bread for the family.

As hundreds of Union soldiers were gathering on Cemetery Hill, the Rebs began a systematic house-to-house search for any Union soldiers who had been cut off and were hiding everywhere in Gettysburg. For the rest of the evening the Rebs collected prisoners, including old John Burns, who with no fewer than three wounds on his body, was nearly hung as a soldier out of uniform. After a somewhat lengthy speech by Burns, who could talk a bear out of a tree, he was freed and allowed to go home lick his wounds in the basement cellar.

All through Gettysburg, triumphant Rebs were laughing and singing, amid the debris of rifles, cartridge cases, and clothing. Bodies, both north and south, littered yards, streets, alleys, and homes. For the most part, the dead Union soldiers had been stripped almost to nakedness.

As evening approached it became apparent to Jennie that Georgia's little red brick house, sought out as a haven of safety, turned out to be quite the opposite. The Wade family now found themselves in the middle of no-man's land between the two great armies. The dead and wounded from the first days fighting lay in the field on the east side of the house as well as in front. The cries of the wounded could be heard in-between the bedlam of the earsplitting noise of combat.

When Jennie and Harry came in the house for the night they found the side table stacked with 10 loaves of fresh bread. Mary Wade was cleaning the kitchen table off getting ready for supper.

"Now don't you be givin out any more bread," Mary Wade cautioned. "Kin is closer than strangers."

"I know. But you also know what the Good Book says about helping those in need," Jennie rebuffed. "We have more than we will need. I can't see any harm in giving a hand to those poor boys," Jennie said looking at her mother.

Mary Wade did not respond to Jennie's comments and went into the parlor to check on Georgia and the baby. Jennie and Harry followed.

"How is the baby?" Jennie asked Georgia as she walked over and gently caressed his head as the baby nursed.

"He's doing just fine, Aunt Jennie. Just fine," Georgia stated. "He is hungry all the time."

"I heard from some of the soldiers today that the entire town, except for the southern end near the Cemetery, was controlled by the Rebs. It's unbelievable. Just can't believe this has happened," Jennie moaned.

"I know. We never would have thought such a terrible situation as this would have happened in our town. We were all so hopeful yesterday when General Buford's men rode through town with people singing patriotic songs and all. Now it seems like the end of the world," Georgia lamented.

The wounded were found everywhere throughout the town, and by evening, the Lutheran Seminary building, the college, churches, all public buildings, and even some homes were converted into hospitals. Unfortunately, there were so many wounded that many would lie for days where they fell until the battle was over.

After an hour of enduring the moaning sounds of the wounded outside the house, Harry ran downstairs and asked if he and Isaac could sleep in the parlor. Jennie brought down the trundle beds and placed the boys on the floor next to the parlor door. Before the boys went back to sleep Jennie placed her arms around each boy and asked God's protection on the family. Mary Wade reclined on the bed with

Georgia while Jennie rested on the horsehair lounge under the window at the north end of the house.

Jennie could not sleep as she listened to the cries of the wounded, and the occasional rifle crack outside the house. Her thoughts turned to Jack. I wonder if he is here in town? Is he wounded? Will he stop by the house and find I am not there? Maybe I need to go back to my house on Breckenridge and wait for Jack? If I can, tomorrow I will walk back to the house and leave Jack a note of my where abouts.

Jennie listened to the ticking of the mantel clock and the continued muffled moaning of the wounded.

"When the sun comes up tomorrow, no one knows what the day will bring," she whispered. "Only Gods knows. Or does He? Is God too far away to see all of this pain and suffering down here?" Jennie questioned, as sleep finally came to her. Tonight, God seemed so far away.

Tomorrow the Rebs will be gone and Jack will come home. Tomorrow will be a better day. I am sure tomorrow God would feel closer; Jennie was sure of it.

11
The Second Day
July 2, 1863

The sun rose around 4:30 on Thursday in a rose-colored sky. The air around Gettysburg was sultry, and a light fog settled along the ground. The Wade family had slept very little. Situated immediately between the Rupp Tannery building and the Union fortifications at the bottom of the hill, the little red brick house was an ideal cover for Union sharpshooters who had moved into position throughout the night.

The soldiers could hide behind the south side of the house, look around the corner, and fire their weapons. This accounted for the numerous dead and wounded men around the house when Jennie looked out of the window around six. She had taken a great risk in exposing her head in the window because the house had already lost three window panes due to minie balls. Jennie quickly left the window when sniper fire resumed toward the foot of Cemetery Hill.

The industrialized area of Gettysburg was at the south end. The largest parcel of industry was made up of the Wagon Hotel and a large parking area for customer's wagons. Jennie could see the snipers down the street in the hotel; the soldiers positioned themselves in the windows and at holes punched in the hotel's roof, giving them an advantage at shooting down on the Rebs. Periodically there would be a thud on the side of Georgia's house as a lead ball struck the brick.

As she was watching the soldiers in the hotel windows Jennie noticed all the shutters in the front of the house were still opened.

"Mother, we need to close the shutters in the front, I guess we forgot to close the shutters yesterday in all the excitement."

"No, Jennie! Not now! The firing has picked up in the last several minutes, making it just too dangerous to go outside," Mrs. Wade advised in a stern voice as she walked back into the parlor to help wash the baby.

By 6:30, the Confederates stationed in the Rupp Tannery building began a fusillade of shots in the direction of Georgia's house. As Jennie was having her morning devotions at the kitchen table she could again hear the thud of lead striking the house. It was a sound Jennie could not get used to and a sound she would never forget. As she was concluding her devotions with a prayer, a loud knock on the kitchen door startled her.

"Who would be knocking on a door in the middle of a battle?" she yelled out to her mother and sister who were in the parlor with the baby and the boys, who were still sleeping.

"Could it be Jack? Yes, it is. It has to be Jack," she mused to herself.

Slowly Jennie opened the door with caution, hoping she would see Jack standing there smiling. She remembered every detail of what he looked like on their last evening together.

Disappointment flooded her soul when the man standing in the door turned out to be a wounded Union soldier. His shoulder and arm were covered in blood and there was dried blood over his shaggy bearded face. His blue uniform was torn and muddy.

Jennie wanted to shut the door rather than deal with the results of this war. She hated the war and everything the war stood for. Wounded soldiers were everywhere but this one came to her door. Why?

"This could be Jack," she whispered to herself looking intently at his shoulder wound. What if Jack had been wounded and stood on some farm porch right now asking for help. Would Jack be turned away? Jennie questioned herself silently as she motioned for the soldier to come in.

"Let's have a look at that shoulder of yours." Jennie stated as he sat down at the kitchen table. She went to the stairway cabinets and brought over an old sheet.

"I thank thee kindly, Miss. You're a God-sent angel. Yes, you are. All I really wanted was some bread. A wounded friend of mine who died yesterday just behind your house here said you gave him and some other soldiers bread yesterday afternoon. Said it was good. Yes indeed." His voice sounded so much like Jack's voice. After the soldier removed his shirt and the wound was cleaned Jennie discovered to the soldier's joy it was only a flesh wound.

"Looks like you are going to make it, soldier. Probably will die an old grandpa with your grandchildren playing around your feet on the porch," Jennie chuckled. "What's your name, soldier?

"John Tandy, Miss, I was with the 11th Corps yesterday afternoon when our lines crumbled and we sort of retreated out of there fast-like and fetched our way to this here hill behind you. Don't believe there are many left in my unit. By God's grace I am here on this side of eternity," John said, as he rubbed his calloused hands.

"I do believe you are going to live to fight another day, soldier. Have you heard anything on the 87th Pennsylvania? Or of a battle fought at Winchester, Virginia?" she questioned in a serious voice.

"No Miss can't say I knowed that-there 87th you're talking about. Or that battle," he said shaking his head. Although Jennie showed no disappointment, her heart sank with his words.

"Do thee have kin in that there company, Miss?" he questioned in a raspy voice.

Jennie quickly looked the other way as she fought back a flood of tears. The soldier sensed he asked a hurting question, and remained quiet as he adjusted his shoulder bandage.

"Yes. I do have a loved one in the 87th and I thought his company would be here in Gettysburg fighting."

The soldier got up slowly from the table and walked toward the door. Reaching the door he turned and said in a sympathetic voice, "I pray to God your loved one is safe from harm. This here war is a terrible war, and we all pray someday it will be over soon. God go with you, Miss."

Once outside, he ran around the corner of the house just as a minie ball missed his head and sank deep into the brick wall with a thud.

"That is one lucky soldier," Jennie exclaimed. "One lucky soldier indeed!"

"Mary Virginia Wade! Why in tar nation are you standing in the doorway? Are you trying to be a target for some Reb who has poor eyesight and can't see you are a woman standing at the door?" Mary Wade shouted.

"I was just watching the soldier leave," Jennie retorted. "That soldier has been very lucky so far, Mother."

"I was just wondering why you were standing in the doorway, when a few minutes ago you were concerned about rushing outside and closing the shutters," Mary Wade said in a tense voice.

"I'm sorry! The soldier needed help and I helped him."

Jennie's mother placed her hand on Jennie's arm. "I'm sorry I spoke so harshly. I believe we are all under a lot of tension cooped up here in the house. We hope and pray every day is the last day of this fighting going on around us."

Jennie went into the parlor to see if Georgia needed anything. Her baby was nursing, snuggled in his mother's arms safe and warm from the death and destruction surrounding the house.

"When John is finished nursing I will rock him for a while and give you some time to yourself," Jennie suggested.

"I think he's ready now," Georgia said wiping his little mouth and then handing him over to her sister. Jennie sat in the corner rocker as she sang softly to her nephew.

Georgia assisted her mother in the kitchen while they prepared another 10 loaves of bread. As Jennie completed her song she noticed how quiet it had become outside the house. Except for distant gunfire, the silence outside the house was eerie. Jennie looked at the mantel clock, as it struck 12:00 noon.

Jennie was just about ready to go outside and close the shutters when at 1:00, the patter of the deadly lead minie balls began striking the house. The air was filled with one tremendous boom after another. Then began the screaming sounds of artillery shells passing over the house, increasing with every passing minute.

Mary Wade gathered her family into the parlor and made everyone sit on the floor. Georgia had the nursing baby cradled in her arms next to Jennie. In between the passing of the artillery shells, the family could hear the baby making sucking sounds, which was a very different contrast to the shelling.

Around 2:00 in the afternoon, a 10-pound. Parrot shrapnel shell fired from Oak Ridge, north of town, came crashing through the slant roof, creating the loudest noise anyone in the house had ever heard. The boys screamed at the sound of splintering wood and falling bricks, and rushed under Georgia's bed at the same time Jennie fainted. Mary Wade brought Jennie some water and held her head up to drink. Georgia lay on her side covering her baby with her body while the boys continued screaming.

After a few hours the shelling stopped. Mary Wade and Jennie ascended the narrow stairway to investigate the damage upstairs. The artillery shell had passed through the slanted, wooden-shingled roof over the north stairway, and then proceeded through the plaster wall dividing the double dwelling. The Parrot shell created a hole in the brick wall close to one foot in diameter.

"I cannot believe a shell can create a hole so large," Jennie said. "It is amazing!" She walked over to the hole and was startled to see Catharine McClain, the widowed lady who lived on the south side of the double, looking back.

"Blessed sweet Jesus. What grace He gives to us!" Catharine declared.

"Are you folks well over there?" she questioned in a concerned voice, fanning the dust away from her face.

"Yes we are, Mrs. McClain!" Jennie answered quickly. "We were downstairs in the parlor when the shell struck. Where did it go?" Jennie questioned, looking around the room.

Mrs. McClain pointed to the wall on the southwest corner. "I believe the shell entered in the wall over there and then pierced the roof again as it continued through the other side of the house. Blessed sweet Jesus; the shell did not explode!"

Jennie felt sorry for Mrs. McClain, who had lost her husband in Virginia a few weeks ago. The story was sad because the 34-year-old Catharine was left with four children to raise by herself.

"Thank you Jennie for asking how I am doing. God was truly with us all when the shell struck the house and failed to explode," she paused and looked over to the corner when the shell entered the wall. "We all deal the best we can with whatever God hands out to us on this side of eternity. He is good to us," Mrs. McClain testified.

As Jennie was talking to Mrs. McClain, Harry and Georgia came to see what happened upstairs. When Harry saw the large hole in the wall, the first thing he wanted to do was climb through the hole.

"You just stop right there Harry," Mrs. Wade barked as she grabbed his shirt. "The wall could fall down on you and crush your head," she said as she shooed him downstairs.

Jennie was beginning to wonder if the family should continue to stay on the first floor or go down to the cellar.

"What do you think?" Jennie questioned her mother and sister as they descended the stairway. "Would it be safer in the cellar?"

"I don't believe the cellar would be good for the baby. Too damp and musty," Georgia protested. "Besides this battle should be over soon and we have all been safe so far."

"The failure of that shell not exploding within our house was a miracle sent from God," Mary Wade advised. "God will continue to protect us." Jennie and Georgia nodded their approval.

Throughout the day, soldiers took a chance and knocked on the front door, requesting bread and water as lead minie balls struck the house. By five p.m. the bread was gone and Jennie started the yeast for another six loaves. The dough was mixed into sponge and then left to rise until the morning. Jennie wanted to make sure they would have enough bread for any more soldiers who would come to the door.

As darkness approached, the artillery and small arms fire subsided. Except for the occasional picket fire, all was quiet. Jennie turned down the oil lamp on the kitchen table and cracked open the kitchen door. She had to have fresh air. Her thoughts rested on Jack, and she longed to be in his arms. The air surrounding the house was thick with a haze of smoke and Jennie could only make out dark forms lying about in the field in front of the house. Either the soldiers were dead, or so severely wounded they could not move.

There was an eerie calmness in the air as Jennie closed the door. She noticed there were two bullet holes at the top of the solid oak door and the sight of the holes sent cold shudders through her body. She quickly locked the door and went into the parlor where her family was already asleep.

Jennie sat down on the lounge sofa under the north window and leaned her head back.

"It can't be much longer," she said to herself. "A person would think with all of this lead flying around our town over the last several days, the armies would be running out of ammunition soon," she whispered to herself as sleep slowly enveloped her.

Around two in the morning Jennie awoke to the sound of rifle fire behind the house and could not get back to sleep. She got up and went into the kitchen. Even with the sporadic rifle fire, she felt safe enough to open the kitchen door and step outside into the coolness of the night air.

She walked a short distance to where a group of wounded soldiers were gathered. When the soldiers saw her walking toward them they asked for water or bread. Jennie went to the windless pump and carried back two buckets of water for the wounded.

Jennie sat down alongside one the soldiers who had just received some water. In the dim moonlight, she could make out that he was an officer, but she did not know what rank.

"Thanks for the water, ma'am," the soldier moaned.

"I just wish I could do more for you boys. There's just too many of you to tend to at once."

"Be quiet," the soldier whispered. "Them Rebs over yonder can hear real good at night," he stated, as he nodded his head toward the tannery buildings down from the house. "Women or not, them Rebs will shoot you dead right here and now because they be real good sharpshooters," he warned.

"If you don't mind, sir, I have one question for you," Jennie asked politely.

"You go right ahead Miss, with your question," the officer wheezed in a soft horse voice.

"Do you know if the 87th Pennsylvania is fighting here? I know someone who is with the 87th that I am concerned about and haven't heard from him for over a month," she questioned.

"Miss, can't say I know anything at all about the 87th. I am with the 73rd Pennsylvania, company B." The soldier paused for a moment.

"Now, we did hear-tell of a battle fought somewhere around Winchester, Virginia, a few weeks ago that turned into another disaster for us. That's all I know."

Jennie squeezed his hand. "May God go with you, soldier."

"And with you too, Miss."

Jennie wanted to cry, not so much for this poor bleeding soldier lying at her feet but for the countless nameless soldiers killed over the last several days that will leave a loved one behind. As far as Jennie was concerned the anguish, pain and separation of battle robbed the war of the honor and glory so many young men sought after.

12
The Third Day
July 3, 1863

Jennie had gotten up before the first streaks of light filtered through the eastern sky. She could tell it was going to be a hot and humid day; the thermometer outside the kitchen window already read 75 degrees. She wanted to bring firewood and water into the house as soon as possible before the fighting continued. She woke Harry at the same time she got up, to assist her in the wood and water gathering.

When Harry opened the kitchen door he was besieged with the cries for water from the wounded soldiers who had gathered around the house for safety. After gathering water for the family, Jennie had Harry carry buckets of water to the wounded soldiers close to the house.

"Don't you go too far from the walls of the house? Remember Harry, the Rebs at this distance, cannot tell if you are a civilian or a young boy soldier," Jennie cautioned Harry. "As soon as daylight breaks you fetch yourself in the house right away. Do you understand?"

"Yes, Jennie," Harry snapped back at his sister while holding a bucket of water.

Jennie returned to the warm, sultry kitchen and with the mixing tray, began mounding the dough until it was stiff, and then left the dough to rise again.

The day was going to be long and sticky, she thought to herself as she wiped away the perspiration on her forehead. After she finished cleaning the top of the dough tray, someone knocked on the kitchen door.

"Is that you, Harry?" Jennie questioned.

"No, Miss. This is just another hungry soldier asking for a few crumbs of bread and some water," he muttered.

With caution Jennie cracked open the door. "Sir, if you could please come back later in the afternoon we will have some more freshly baked bread. For now we are all out of bread."

"Thank you, Miss. I will come back later," the soldier said in a polite voice, then tipped his cap and disappeared around the corner of the house.

Just as Jennie was closing the door, Harry came running in. "I was only able to feed a few soldiers, Jennie. We just plum ran out of bread and we..." Harry was interrupted as a kitchen windowpane was shot out, sending glass shards everywhere across the kitchen floor. They both fell to the floor on the glass, and stayed down with their hands over their heads. They could hear the thud of lead as the minie balls began striking the north side of the house.

Harry managed to close the door with his foot. They both helped each other up and then wiped the glass from their clothes. Jennie could see by his ashen-white face that he was a scared little child. Then, again, Jennie was just as scared, too.

"That was a close call, don't you think, Harry?" Jennie remarked, trying to bolster his spirits.

Before Harry could answer, a terrible cannonading began over by Culp's Hill. The house shook, lifting everyone out of their beds. In a matter of minutes artillery shells began to screech over the house making that whistling sound the family was all too familiar with. The exploding artillery shells east of the house caused the house to rumble and Georgia's baby, along with Isaac, began to cry.

The boys wanted to go down into the root cellar to get away from the deafening noise. Mary Wade thought about the shell that went through the roof yesterday and felt the boys were right. But, she would not take a chance with everyone going out the kitchen door and down into the root cellar in the middle of a battle.

Georgia went into the parlor and began rocking the baby, hoping to calm him down. Mary Wade sat on the floor with the boys on either side of her, and Jennie rested on the sofa lounge under the north window and began her morning devotions. After a brief prayer, she opened the Bible to the 27th Psalm, taking comfort in the words.

Wesley Culp had returned to his hometown on July 1st with his Company in the 2nd Virginia Infantry. Wesley's company was positioned on Brinkerhoff's Ridge, which lay northeast along Hanover Road. Wesley had hoped to see Jennie Wade on the first day they arrived in Gettysburg. However, after he made his way to her house on Breckenridge Street, he found out that Jennie and her family were gone. The only occupants were a few Reb sharpshooters who had taken up positions in the upstairs rooms.

Wesley learned from the next-door neighbor, Ben Harden, where Jennie had gone on the morning of July 1st. After talking to the soldiers gathered in front of the house, Wesley found out where the Confederate line extended. Unfortunately for Jennie, Georgia's house, "the little red brick house with the white picket fence," was just in front of the Union line.

Wesley traversed down Baltimore Pike, staying close to the buildings, and crossed Winebrenner's run to the Tannery Building; the furthest position of the Confederate front. He could see the little red brick structure from the upstairs window and knew it would be certain death if he tried to run to the house. He figured he could wait it out. There would be plenty of time to see Jennie once the Blue Bellies were driven out of Gettysburg.

In the late afternoon on July 2nd, Wesley did manage to obtain permission from his commanding officer to visit his sister's house well within the Confederate lines of battle. The house was located on West Middle Street across from Jack's parents. His older sister, Barbara "Annie" Myers and younger sister, Julia, along with his Aunt Maggie Myers, were shocked and surprised to see Wesley standing at their door. They all stood there for a few moments looking at this short, husky, sun-bronzed soldier in a tattered butternut uniform standing before them.

The situation was awkward. Even if the man standing before them was kin, he was still the "enemy." After a few moments, the silence was broken when his Aunt Maggie said, "You know Wesley, there are some in our family that have threatened to shoot you on sight if they ever see you again! Providence is with you tonight because none of them are here."

"I know them are not idle words," Wesley agreed sleeplessly. "I know how my uncles felt about me going south and all. They never could understand why I had to go with my work when the business was moved to Shepherdstown. I reckon I don't ever expect them to understand."

She gave him a strong hug and ushered him into the parlor, where Wesley shared the story about Jack's mortal wound and the dictated letter from the hospital bed. He slowly removed the letter from his jacket and showed them the sealed yellow paper with the letter to Jennie enclosed.

The family coaxed and begged him throughout the evening to give them the letter.

"It is just a precaution, Wesley. Just in case you cannot make it back to the house," Julia stated.

"Yes, just a precaution. Maybe you could at least share the contents of the letter with us so when we see Jennie Wade we can share Jack's last message," his Aunt Maggie coaxed.

"No! I promised Jack I would fetch the letter to Jennie and no one else. And Aunt Maggie you know better than to ask a man not to go back on his word," Wesley said in a firm voice to his aunt.

"I can tell you all that probably Jack Skelly died of his wounds a few days later. They would have buried him in the Winchester area."

Julia and Annie began crying. They had been friends of the Skellys for years, and even with death surrounding them every day in Gettysburg the news of the death of a close personal friend was always hard to fathom.

"If for some reason I do not make it to Jennie's house with the letter could you…would you… let the Skelly family and the Wades know what happened to Jack?" Wesley sighed as he wiped the tears from his cheeks with his sleeve. "I hate this war!"

"Yes, Wesley we will inform both families about the death of Jack. You take care of yourself. God bless you," Aunt Maggie sobbed.

Wesley embraced his family, then turned and walked out the door trying to hide his flood of tears, which he could not control.

Wesley spent the evening on the ridge with his company. Around two in the morning of July 3rd, his unit left Brinkerhoff's Ridge and moved to the west side of Rock Creek. At Rock Creek his company joined Johnson's division on the slope overlooking Culp's Hill. He looked across Rock Creek at his cousin's Henry's farm with its rock-covered slopes and beautiful trees.

"How could I have ended up here?" he said to himself. "Imagine that, right back where I started from years ago in my childhood. Who would have ever thought this would happen."

Memories flooded his mind as he looked into the distance and saw the old swimming hole in Rock Creek. It was there, long ago, that he and his brothers would swim away the lazy, hot July afternoons.

"Oh, those were the days," Wesley said out loud to himself. "Those were the days!"

Grimy and unshaven, Wesley bowed his head there in the freshly dug trench. Even though many of his fellow soldiers were around him, he felt increasingly alone. As he looked up and down the shallow trench he noticed each soldier braced himself for what they all knew was going to be a losing fight up the hill. Some prayed. Many wrote letters and pinned them on their jackets with their name for burial identification. Some just sat there smoking and blankly stared out across the open valley to the slope of the hill.

Wesley said a brief prayer and then, with his eyes closed, readied himself for the charge across his beloved Rock Creek and then up the slope of his cousin's hill. In the dim distance, he could see his Captain moving among the corporals and sergeants of his company giving out orders.

"It won't be long now," Wesley remarked to himself. "It's just unbelievable. It's just unbelievable!" He whispered under his breath.

Jennie completed the 27th Psalm and started reading the 28th Psalm out loud. "'Unto thee will I cry, O Lord my rock; be not silent to me; least, if thou be silent to me, I become like them that go down into the pit.'" She paused and looked out the window thinking the fighting had stopped because of the stillness surrounding the house.

Jennie wiped her brow and continued reading. "'Hear the voice of my supplications, when I cry unto thee, when I lift...'"

"Mother! Would you please ask Jennie to stop reading aloud. I don't want the baby awake and crying. Please!" Georgia snapped in an irritable voice.

Jennie stopped immediately, not wanting to increase the tension in the house, and placed her Bible on the stand next to the sofa.

Around seven a.m. the sharpshooters at the Rupp Tannery office building began firing at the Union soldiers at the foot of Cemetery Hill behind Georgia's house.

Just as Jennie left the sofa, a minie ball smashed through the front window and struck the southwest bedpost just a few feet from where Georgia and her baby were lying. The lead ball went through the bedpost, hit the wall, and finally fell on the bed. Both women screamed, bringing Mary Wade in from the kitchen to investigate. The lead ball was still warm when Mary Wade gathered up the lead and the wood splinters from the bedpost.

Jennie suggested that Georgia and the baby get down on the floor with their brother and Isaac for safety until this new outbreak of shooting was over. After helping cover the baby, who was still sleeping in spite of the noise, Jennie went into the kitchen to help her mother.

"If there is anyone in this house that is going to be killed today, I hope it is me, because Georgia has that little baby," Jennie said to her mother.

The preparatory work for making biscuits was begun by Jennie. She went over to her mixing tray and prepared the flour and baking soda for the biscuits. Jennie moved the mixing tray off the kitchen table and carried the tray to a plank-bottom chair in the southwest corner of the kitchen. She would feel safer there, she thought. The outside door was closed and locked, and the solid oak door into the parlor was opened, giving her double protection.

Just before eight o'clock, the sound of artillery shells over the house stopped, and except for the intermittent sniping of the sharpshooters, an ominous silence prevailed in the house. For the first time in days, all was quiet.

For a brief moment, Jennie thought she heard a bird singing. She shook her head thinking that no bird could have lived through the rain of lead that has passed through the sky in and around Gettysburg over the last several days. She looked up at the kitchen clock; the time was eight o'clock.

"Maybe today," she said to herself as she began to kneading the dough. "Maybe today I will see Jack. When the Rebs leave he will come. I know he will!"

Jennie paused from her kneading and wiped the perspiration from her brow.

Won't that be wonderful when Jack comes home and we are together again, she thought, looking at the clock again.

"Its 8:15, Mother," Jennie, remarked. "We need to get the fire built up for baking."

As they worked together in the kitchen, the room became silent, and except for the crackling fire in the oven nothing could be heard. The silence was eerie, especially after three days of the continual noise of battle. Both mother and daughter could feel and sense the calmness surrounding them.

Jennie felt content with her life and she was at peace with God. After all, what more can anyone asks for in this life but to find complete happiness in someone you love. She and Jack had their time, and it was a wonderful dance she thought as she continued working with the dough.

Motion and time began to slow down as Jennie slowly looked up at her mother and smiled. Her mother returned the smile.

Everything in the room came to a standstill as if suspended in time for Jennie. Even the ticking of the wall clock was suspended in time and slowed down. Tick...tock, tick...tock, tick...tock, tick. The clock stopped as a sudden pain pierced her back and all became black.

Jennie never heard the deadly lead messenger that ushered her into eternity. It was swift. It was sudden. It was forever. With a loud crash the minie ball had penetrated the outside oak door, and continued through the panel of the inside parlor door and struck Jennie full in her back. The lead ball entered below her left shoulder blade and continued through her heart, coming to rest in her corset at the front of her body. Jennie never gave out a sigh, or a good-bye. Not a word of her departure to anyone, she was just gone in a moment.

Mrs. Wade turned when she heard Jennie's body hit the floor.

"Oh my God! No! No! This can't be? Not my Jennie!" She rushed over to where Jennie was lying in a pool of blood with her hands still covered with dough.

In total shock and with little emotion Mrs. Wade announced the terrible news to Georgia in the parlor. "Georgia, your sister is dead."

At the horrible painful news about her sister Georgia began screaming. The boys heard the news at the same time Georgia did and they began crying. Mrs. Wade gathered the boys on the bed with their sister and wrapped her arms around them.

A few moments later, two Union soldiers broke open the front door. They had heard Georgia's screaming and feared someone had been killed in the house. Two other soldiers came from the upstairs. The presence of these soldiers was a total mystery to Mrs. Wade and Georgia, as they did not know how the two men gained entry into the house or how long they had been upstairs. They appeared to belong to a company of sharpshooters stationed around the house over the last several days.

The first two soldiers examined Jennie's body behind the parlor door and confirmed she was dead. After a brief discussion among themselves the soldiers decided the family should take refuge in the cellar on the south side of the house. The two soldiers who had been upstairs suggested they enlarge the hole created by the shell, and then move the family to the safety in the south cellar.

When the expansion of the hole was completed, the family was gathered together, along with a few of their belongings.

Mrs. Wade could not bear to leave Jennie's body alone in the kitchen, and requested the soldiers carry Jennie to the south cellar. Mrs. Wade had been with her daughter her entire life and wanted them to be together in the end.

Outside the house the shelling continued, as the noise of battle grew louder. The soldiers covered Jennie's body with a quilt Georgia had made years ago in anticipation of her wedding day.

Georgia and the baby were the first to pass through the enlarged hole. A soldier helped her as another soldier carried the baby gently in his arms. Following Georgia and the baby was another soldier carrying a split-bottom rocker. Above the roof they could hear the continued whistling shells pass over to their deadly destination. Mrs. Wade followed the soldier with the rocking chair. She refused any assistance as she bent down and passed through the hole on her own. Harry followed his mother, while a soldier carried Isaac.

Reaching the cellar on the south side of the house, they all had a first-hand experience of what a battle is about, with deafening sounds and acrid smoke. As they walked to the cellar steps, Georgia noticed the beautiful garden filled with flowers and greens was no longer there.

The family entered the south cellar in silence. Catharine McClain and her four children were waiting for them. Georgia and Mrs. Wade were heavy with the grief as they entered the basement, not only because of Jennie's untimely death, but also regret that the family had not moved down there on the first day of the battle like Jennie wanted them to. No one had to say a thing. They all knew Jennie would still be alive if they would have listened to Jennie's request on the first day.

After everyone was safe in the cellar, two soldiers went back to the kitchen and carried Jennie's quilt-wrapped body over to the cellar.

They placed her gently on a crock table in the southwest corner of the cellar.

Georgia began rocking her baby, and Mrs. Wade sat down next to her daughter's body and kept a vigil. The boys sat down on the fireplace hearthstone with the McClain children and cried.

"Ladies if you would not mind, we would like to keep guard over the cellar until things quiet down outside," one of the soldiers asked.

Mary Wade did not answer but continued to look at Jennie lying there on the table. Georgia looked up at the soldiers and nodded her head that it would be all right to stand guard.

Around one p.m. Mary Wade decided to go back up-stairs to the kitchen and finish the biscuits and bread Jennie had promised to the soldiers. The soldiers tried to talk her out of going, but they did not know how stubborn she could be.

She completed 10 loaves of bread and biscuits for the soldiers. She then scrubbed the kitchen floor trying to remove Jennie's blood. When they moved back into the house she did not want the blood-soaked floor to remind the family of Jennie's death. Outside the house, the greatest artillery barrage ever fired on this continent began. Even down in the cellar the occupants could hear the deafening, earsplitting rumble of the cannons.

Two cannons near the peach orchard opened fire in rapid succession at the signal for the entire line of cannons to begin. The cannons were fired in salvos and in succession; the air above Gettysburg soon filled with gray smoke and gray dust, which darkened the skies. For hours the ground trembled and men shook in fear.

It was the worst afternoon and night the Wade family could ever remember. The boys slept on their trundle beds, which the soldiers had brought over in the early evening. Georgia slept in the rocker cradling her baby, and Mary Wade sat on the bench next to Jennie, continuing her death vigil. Occasionally she would reach out and hold her daughter's cold and lifeless hand. Jennie would be missed.

The brothers lost a sister who cared for and loved them, a sister who wanted their lives to be better than her life was.

Georgia lost a sister who was closer than a friend and companion, who shared laughter, tears, pain, and sorrows. Mary Wade lost a kind, self-sacrificing daughter, who would always look out for others, first. Jennie would be missed.

The moon refused to shine that night creating a thick darkness over the land. Gettysburg, as well as the rest of the country lost many of its finest youth throughout the day. As the thick darkness covered the town, it also covered the sorrow, loss, pain and the shame that war always brings with it.

The Wade family and the country would never be the same again. Many lives had been changed forever.

13
The Garden
July 4, 1863

A dreary, detached stillness hung over Gettysburg as the morning light pierced the gray darkness. The sky was overcast and ominous; it looked as if it could rain at any moment. A foreboding spirit glazed the atmosphere; the citizens of Gettysburg could sense the foreboding spirit everywhere. The ground was covered with a smoky haze and the air was permeated with a mixture of wood smoke and the stench of rotting flesh of the unburied men and horses scattered across the fields and woods. Here and there were smoldering fires, obscuring one's view of the destruction.

As daylight overcame the darkness, the town, as well as the surrounding countryside, was shrouded in an eerie silence suspended in time. It felt as if the citizens of Gettysburg were awaiting the Fourth Horsemen of the Biblical apocalypse to appear. As for the thousands that lay on the fields and in the woods dead, the pale horse of death had already passed by.

To many of Gettysburg residents, dawn was the beginning of the judgment day; there seemed to be no end to the death and destruction surrounding the town. To the few doctors in both armies, it was the beginning of an overwhelming nightmare. To the hundreds of burial parties, the fields and woods for miles became a hodgepodge cemetery of backbreaking work. To the town undertakers, the aftermath was a bonanza, a gold mine for the taking. To the 22,000 wounded in the town, on the roads, in the ditches, among the rocks, in the woods and across the fields of the battlefield, it was a living hell; a hell where many would lie for days before receiving help. To the Wade family, it was a painful void never again to be filled. And for everyone, the war was an eternal abyss of emptiness.

Around noon, a light drizzle began to fall from a gray-black sky. The drizzle continued until one o'clock, and then a torrential rain descended upon the area. It was as if the heavens wanted to wash away the blood, destruction, and death. The rain came down in blinding sheets and began to flow into the small streams and creeks. In many areas the water ran blood red. Rock Creek very quickly began to flow over its banks and drowned some of the wounded that had sought the solace of the creek for water.

One of the Confederate soldiers mortally wounded was Wesley Culp. Wesley's battered body lay somewhere opposite McAllister's Woods in the Culp's Hill area in a fresh shallow grave.

A close friend, Benjamin Pendleton, who knew where the family lived, told of Wesley's death to his sisters and aunt on the evening of July 3rd. Benjamin was an orderly in the Stonewall Brigade and helped bury his friend Wesley. Benjamin, along with his company, was retreating north of Gettysburg and had the opportunity to pay his respects to Wesley's family.

Benjamin explained to the family where Wesley's shallow grave could be found.

"We buried our friend next to a large crooked oak tree close to Culp's Hill to make it easier for you folks to find. We wanted Wesley to have a decent burial. You folks know how he could be. You know, he always wanted to go his own way.

Wesley was killed instantly as he peered over a large rock to see what was going on across Rock Creek." The young soldier paused as he wiped away tears from his face with his sleeve. "There was just something about that creek that had a place in his past, or who knows what."

The young soldier again paused trying to hold back the tears welling up in his eyes. "We tried to stop him from looking over that-there rock, knowing sharpshooters were positioned on the hill. He just wouldn't listen to us."

"Sad. So sad. We all enjoyed his company and friendship. Most of our friends are gone now. I reckon there are only three of us left out of the 15 in the company from two years ago," Benjamin said shaking his head.

By now everyone in the room was in tears. News like this would be a sorrowful pain experienced by thousands of families over the next several weeks, as the tragedy of Gettysburg became known across the country.

As soon as the weather broke and the family felt it would be safe to cross the battlefield, they traveled out to the McAllister's Woods area to retrieve Wesley's body and give him a decent burial. There were shallow graves everywhere. Many of the graves were becoming uncovered as the rains washed the dirt away, exposing the gruesome sight of hands and legs and an occasional head sticking up through the mud.

The grieving family looked for hours in the rain. The only evidence of Wesley Culp they could find was his gunstock carved with W.C. The gunstock was found along Rock Creek among other battlefield materials such as canteens, clothing leather belts and shoes of every description.

With the disappearance of Wesley's body, the letter to Jennie from Jack Skelly was forever gone. All three-childhood friends would soon be united in death; each one losing their life through the Confederate invasion into the North.

Early on the afternoon of July 4th, General Lee began his orderly retreat back to Virginia. The wagon train loaded with their supplies and wounded was 17 miles long. Guarded by Imboden's Cavalry, General Lee began his trek through Greenwood. For thousands of the Confederate wounded in the wagons, the journey home was going to be a tortuous one of pain. Very few of the citizens of Gettysburg realized, until later in the day, that the Confederates were leaving their town.

At one o'clock, a few of the Union soldiers that had been positioned around Georgia's home offered to bury Jennie and repair the damage caused by the shell hole in the wall upstairs. As the family came up out of the cellar, their eyes fell upon three dead horses next to the outhouse, which were the victims of shrapnel. Everywhere across the backyard where Georgia looked there were dead and wounded soldiers. It was the sight of these dead and wounded men that prompted Mrs. Wade's decision to stay with Georgia and the baby a few more days.

"Harry, we want you to go and see Mr. Comfort at the Garlach cabinet shop on Baltimore Street; obtain a coffin from him if you can and then return."

During the occupation of the town, the Rebs had taken over the cabinet shop for use in making coffins for their officers. As Harry entered the building, he saw that Mr. Comfort had an uncompleted walnut coffin that had been prepared by the Confederate workman for one of their colonels. However, they left town in such a hurry that they forgot the colonel's coffin.

Mr. Comfort hurriedly completed the coffin and Harry helped him place it onto a wagon. Together they drove down Baltimore Street past and through the many barricades the Rebs had built, to Georgia's home.

Four soldiers brought Jennie out of the cellar and placed her body on top of the coffin. There had been no time for the cleansing, embalming or redressing of the body. As Mrs. Wade was checking Jennie's pockets she found the front door key to their home on

Breckenridge Street and a picture of Jack Skelly.

As Mrs. Wade looked at Jack's picture, an overpowering wave of guilt and remorse flooded her already tear-stained face. It would take a long time for her to forgive herself for her actions and comments about Jack.

Around four o'clock, Samuel, who had spent the last few days in the Pierces' cellar, appeared on the doorstep of Georgia's home. Samuel had heard of Jennie's death from the neighbor, as the news of Gettysburg's only civilian death spread throughout the community.

Jennie was gently placed in the coffin with Georgia's quilt still wrapped around her body. Her hands were still covered with bread dough as a mute testimony of her loyalty to the Union. As the soldiers began nailing the lid on the coffin it was difficult for the battle hardened men not to show any emotion.

The rain had been coming down all afternoon, and the ground had become a quagmire of mud. As the soldiers dug the grave in the southeast corner of Georgia's garden, the sidewalls of the grave kept caving.

Around five in the afternoon, the rain began to fall again as Georgia, Mrs. Wade, Samuel, Harry and six soldiers gathered around the open grave in the garden. There were no spoken prayers and no music as four of the soldiers began lowering the coffin into the muddy hole. The soldiers removed their caps out of respect for the lost heroine.

A few of the soldiers standing around the open grave had been given food and water to drink from Jennie just a few days ago. All of the soldiers had tears in their eyes. Standing there at attention, one of the soldiers said, "God bless you, Miss. May ye rest in peace until the great awakening." The other soldiers whispered, "Amen."

For a few moments everyone stood there in silence around the open grave. The family exhausted and still in shock over Jennie's death, remained silent. Georgia tried to cover her baby's head in the rain. One of the soldiers wanted to keep the baby in the house but Georgia wanted Lewis Kenneth McClellan at his Aunt Jennie's funeral. She wanted him never to forget what had taken place here in the first three days of July in 1863. The story would be passed down from generation to generation.

As the soldiers began filling in the grave, the heavens opened up with a downpour that helped them close the grave. Everyone except the three soldiers who were shoveling the dirt ran into the house, and stood in the doorway under the roof overjet to watch the soldiers complete the job. Even the battle-hardened soldiers were caught up in the emotions of the afternoon.

As they completed their work, a downpour came so hard the freshly dug grave became obscured in the mud of the garden. It seemed that God wanted to cover the tragedy of this young girl from Gettysburg; to wipe away all traces that her needless death ever occurred.

Georgia's garden, which had been so full of beauty and color just a few days ago, was now nothing but a trampled piece of ground covered in mud. As she turned to enter the house Georgia was glad Jennie never saw what the garden looked like today.

Deep in Georgia's heart, she knew the ground now, would always be sacred, and in the coming spring the flowers will grow more beautiful than anywhere on the earth covering the graves of their loved ones.

14
The Promise Kept
November 1867

The day was exceptionally cold as John and Georgia turned off Baltimore Pike and entered the dirt road through the Gatehouse into Evergreen Cemetery. The sky was overcast and the weather felt as if it could snow at any moment. Georgia checked to see if her four-year-old son Lewis was covered properly. The weather had changed for the worse over the last few days, and Georgia was hoping for decent weather as they began their trip to Iowa.

Georgia had wanted John to leave early enough for the train station in order to give them time to make a stop at Jennie's gravesite in Evergreen Cemetery. She wanted to say good-bye to Jennie before they left Gettysburg. All their earthly belongings were already at the train station, packed in crates and loaded on the train. They were both excited about beginning their new life together in Denison, Iowa.

Ever since Jennie had been killed four years ago, Georgia had wanted to leave Gettysburg. There were too many sad memories for her to overcome. John had been discharged from the army and had no desire to reenlist.

After their close friends, the Laubs, moved to Iowa, Georgia saw her chance to leave Gettysburg and begin a new life devoid of the scars of the Civil War.

Since the war, Georgia had been involved with nursing. After the battle in Gettysburg, Georgia served as a part-time nurse assistant to the hundreds of wounded soldiers left by both armies.

She did such a fine job in Gettysburg that the doctors gave her full-time position assisting the wounded at Camp Letterman, two miles outside of Gettysburg. The nursing was exactly what Georgia needed to help her overcome the grief and loss of Jennie. The nursing also kept her active while John was away fighting.

In 1864, Georgia traveled to Washington for a few months of training and nursing in the Emery Hospital under the direction of Annie Wittenmyer, who was in charge of the Sanitary Commission. Like her sister Jennie, Georgia always wanted to help people.

Passing through the Gatehouse, Georgia could not believe that it had been three years since her husband John and brother John James Wade had made arrangements for Jennie's body to be transferred to the Evergreen Cemetery. Time just slipped by so fast, Georgia thought; as she held her son Lewis close to her body to keep him warm.

To be buried in Evergreen is what Jennie wanted. Jennie had made Georgia promise five years ago that if she would die first, Georgia would make sure she would be buried in her beloved Evergreen Cemetery. She wanted to keep her promise to her sister.

Jennie's body remained in the garden grave behind Georgia's house until late January of 1864 and from there, the body was removed to the cemetery of the German Reformed Church on High Street upon the insistence of Mary Wade.

In 1865, after the war, the McClellans and John James Wade purchased a lot in the Evergreen Cemetery. The lot was a beautiful grassy area along the dirt road winding through the cemetery; not too far from the Gatehouse.

Dan Skelly had also wanted his brother Jack moved from a cemetery in Winchester, Virginia, to Gettysburg. In November of 1864, Dan, along with help from his family, brought Jack's remains back to Gettysburg. After his death on July 12, 1863, nine days after Jennie's untimely death, Jack was buried in the Lutheran Cemetery in Winchester where many of the Union soldiers who fought at the battle of Carter's Woods were buried.

The Skelly family all agreed Jack should be brought back, but left the responsibility to Jack's younger brother Dan. Dan had Jack interred in the Evergreen Cemetery because he remembered Jack and Jennie would often meet there for a rendezvous. As fate would have it, the Wades' cemetery lot was about 75 paces from Jack's gravesite. Dan smiled every time he would visit Jennie and Jack thinking how, even in death, the two of them were together. They both would have wanted that, Dan thought.

Georgia became nervous as the buggy turned onto the dirt road that would take them to the gravesite. She had known this cemetery was a favorite meeting place during Jack's last week home before he left in April. As the buggy came to a slow stop alongside Jennie's headstone, which marked the gravesite, Georgia drew in a large breath.

"Are you going to be all right?" John asked in a voice of compassion. "You know, Georgia, I would come along with you if you wanted me to."

"No. Thank you anyway, John. This is something between Jennie and me," Georgia said as she reluctantly handed Lewis over to her husband. She climbed down out of the buggy onto the frozen grass and slowly crossed the few steps to the gravesite. She could see her breath and felt a cold chill pass through her body.

The flowers that Georgia had placed on the grave last month had succumbed to the night frost, turning dark brown and very brittle. She reached down and removed them from the bronze vase. She felt bad she had not brought flowers to replace the old ones, but it was just the wrong time of the year for fresh flowers. Jennie always like fresh flowers with lots of color and sweet smells that wafted through the house. Georgia had made sure Jennie's grave had fresh flowers every week when her garden was bursting with fragrances and bright colors.

For a few minutes, Georgia stood there looking down at the cold, brown grass covering the grave where Jennie slept. She looked across the cemetery and noted how everything was barren and bleak. She began to shiver, standing still in the bitter air where even her mind seemed frozen.

"Well, Jennie, I believe by now you already know Jack is only a few feet away from you. Seventy-five paces to be exact. Dan Skelly measures 75 paces off every time he comes up to the cemetery to visit you and his brother." Georgia paused to wipe the tears welling up in her eyes.

"I guess you also know that John and I are moving to Iowa. Denison, Iowa. Going to take up nursing there. Life in Gettysburg has never been the same since the war. You know that. I just plain need to move out of the area and go somewhere where there are no remembrances of the war." Georgia stopped and looked over to the buggy where her husband was holding Lewis and laughing, and then back at the gravesite.

"Wasn't fair!" she cried shaking her head. "It wasn't fair! It wasn't fair, Jennie! You were taken way before your time. You were only 20 summers old. It wasn't right. None of it was right. I am still angry with God. I just never could understand why! I can never forgive myself for not insisting we all move to the safety of that root cellar the first day. If we would have gone to the cellar you would still be with us," Georgia sobbed in uncontrolled waves of crying.

"It was my fault! It was all my fault, Jennie! You should not have been there in the kitchen. It was my fault..." Georgia wailed. "Please forgive me for my selfishness for not wanting to go down into the cellar. Your death was all my fault!" she moaned.

After a few minutes she felt a peace come over her, and she managed to control her emotions. It was a peace that flooded her body with forgiveness. Jennie forgave her. And in that moment, God spoke to Georgia's spirit, revealing to her that her sister's untimely death was not her fault. Georgia was free to go. She had made her peace with Jennie, her spirit was set free.

"Life has not been the same since your death and never will be Jennie. You and Jack should have had a wonderful life together, and all of that has been denied the both of you. Jennie, you are loved and missed and will never be forgotten. Never. Mother will bring you fresh flowers in the spring." She paused, wiping her face with a handkerchief.

"Tell Jack we love and miss him too. Good-bye, Jennie, until we meet in the other world." Georgia quickly turned and walked to the waiting buggy.

"Are you going to be alright, Georgia?" "Yes, John everything will be alright."

Lewis noticed that his mother had been crying and wrapped his arms around her. "Don't cry, mama. Don't cry."

As the buggy drove through the Gatehouse, Georgia turned and glanced back toward Jennie's grave. She remembered the words Jennie always recited to her when Georgia felt sad. Georgia wiped her eyes and whispered to Lewis, "Oftentimes, there are hurts, sorrows, and pain, that lie too deep, even for human tears."

The buggy turned sharply onto Baltimore Pike and traveled north to the train station in Gettysburg as Georgia, John, and Lewis began their new life together.

The End

15
Afterward

<u>Mr. James Wade</u>

Mr. Wade was never the same, mentally, after his release from the Eastern Penitentiary where he had spent two years of his life. In January of 1852, his wife, Mary Wade, had James committed to the Adams County Alms House for, as the court records state, "being a lunatic of unsound mind." James spent the remaining years of his life in and out of the Alms House as a sick and broken man. James Wade died in poverty and loneliness at the age of 58 on July 10, 1872. James was buried July 11, 1872 in the Evergreen Cemetery, lot 79, Section A. No one in Gettysburg seemed to realize that he was gone.

<u>Mrs. Mary Wade</u>

Mary Wade was affected the most by the untimely death of her daughter, Jennie. With the death of Jennie Wade, Mary Wade not only lost a kind and loving daughter, but lost the financial support Jennie contributed to the family, in the absence of her father. It would not be until 1871 that Mary Wade would collect $1,440 due to an $8.00 per month pension awarded by Congress for Jennie's service and death while serving in the United States war effort. Mary Wade continued her tailoring business in order to support herself and keep the home on Breckenridge Street; here she lived until her death on December 24, 1892. Mary Wade was buried in the Evergreen Cemetery in the Wade family plot.

Mrs. Georgia Wade McClellan

After the battle of Gettysburg, Georgia served as a nurse to the wounded Union and Confederate soldiers left after both armies had departed. She would leave her baby in the care of her mother during the day, and worked at the Adams Country Court House, which had been converted into a hospital during the battle. When President Lincoln came to Gettysburg on November 18 and 19, 1863, he requested Georgia sit with him on the speakers' platform, in honor of Jennie's sacrifice to the Union, as he delivered the Gettysburg address to the people.

In 1867 the McClellans moved to Denison, Iowa where Georgia practiced nursing for several years. Georgia and John loved children and raised five young ones over the years. Georgia could never forgive herself for Jennie's death. This bitter regret haunted her until she died on September 7, 1927, in Carroll, Iowa. Georgia was 86 years old.

Mr. John Louis McClellan

John McClellan moved his family to Denison, Iowa in 1867 and looked for work, as did his friend H. C. Laub, a carpenter and construction worker. In 1911 he moved his family to Fort Dodge, Iowa, where they ran a small mission house for homeless women. John died March 4, 1913 at Fort Dodge, Iowa, with Georgia at his side.

Samuel S. Wade

Jennie's 12-year-old brother, who was arrested and made a prisoner by the Confederates for trying to save his employer's horse, became a house painter after the war. He married Elizabeth Johns of York Springs, Pennsylvania in 1869, and moved his family to Illinois. Samuel Wade died in 1927 in Peoria, Illinois.

John James Wade

John James was the brother who had his uniform altered on June 26, 1863 and then waved good-bye to Jennie. As her brother left for the war, Jennie commented to her mother she felt she would never see John James again.

He traveled all over the west and ended up in Colorado, where he spent 42 years with his wife Julia and their five children. John James died in Arizona on September 2, 1925.

Harry M. Wade

Eight year-old Harry, who was in the house when his sister Jennie was killed in his early twenties Harry moved to Seattle, Washington where he met the love of his life, Mary. Harry lived the rest of his life in Seattle and on September 26, 1906 he died at the young age of 55.

Lewis Kenneth McClellan

The baby born to Georgia on June 26, 1863, a few days before the battle of Gettysburg, became known as the youngest veteran of the great battle. Both he and his mother survived the three-day siege of the town. Lewis left his family in Iowa and moved to Billings, Montana in 1906, where he died on February 12, 1941 at the ripe old age of 77, one of the last veterans of the Civil War.

Corporal Johnston Hastings Skelly (Jack)

On July 11, 1863, as Jack laid on his deathbed at the Taylor House Hospital in Winchester, Virginia, another personal friend,

John Warner, of the 87th Pennsylvania Infantry, paid him a visit. Jack was delirious and semi-conscious in his final hours, and all John could do was stand alongside Jack's bed and say a brief prayer for his old friend.

On July 12, 1863, Johnston Hastings Skelly passed over into eternity. Jennie Wade had only to wait nine days for Jack. Now, at last, they were both together. Forever.

Yes, there was a time.